C24

THE LONELY MAN

When Harry Hobart, a teacher in a reform school, gets into trouble, he thinks that the police may be after him. He runs away to Yorkshire, buys a caravan and becomes a person 'of no fixed address' . . . In a York pub, Harry encounters Loraine, miserable and suicidal after being jilted. She sticks with him . . . Harry and Loraine are contrasting characters. She thinks he's a fuddy-duddy. He thinks she is over-sophisticated. But as they travel together, they come to admire one another, an admiration which turns into lasting love.

PAUL BLACKDEN

THE LONELY MAN

Complete and Unabridged

LINFORD
Leicester

First published in Great Britain in 1978 by
Robert Hale Limited
London

First Linford Edition
published 2006
by arrangement with
Robert Hale Limited
London

British Library CIP Data

Blackden, Paul
    The lonely man.—Large print ed.—
    Linford romance library
    1. Love stories
    2. Large type books
    I. Title
    823.9'14 [F]

    ISBN 1–84617–180–6

Published by
F. A. Thorpe (Publishing)
Anstey, Leicestershire

Set by Words & Graphics Ltd.
Anstey, Leicestershire
Printed and bound in Great Britain by
T. J. International Ltd., Padstow, Cornwall

This book is printed on acid-free paper

1

Mr Hobart lived such a lonely life he liked to have a meal in a pub occasionally so that he could be with people for a change, and on a Friday in March he was sitting in a corner of *The Pageant* in York eating a pork pie and drinking half a pint of bitter. The bar was crowded with men from the railway offices and some girls from the telephone building nearby and for half an hour Mr Hobart had listened to the chatter and laughter wondering if he could dare get into conversation with anyone. But now it was half-past twelve and he had planned to get to Norfolk by the late afternoon so he finished his pie, drained his glass, and was about to make for the revolving door when through it came a girl who slumped down on the nearest seat and sat staring in front of her looking completely miserable. The girl wore no hat or head scarf and her tawny-yellow hair was almost as short as the boys' at the Reform School. She reminded him of Johnnie whom he had loved so dearly. Johnnie had been miserable too and he wondered what had happened to this girl that she should be so sad. He hoped somebody else would notice her and do something about it, but everyone was busy with their drinking and their gossip, so Mr Hobart, who knew very well that his heart was too big for him, felt he couldn't go away without at least making a gesture of sympathy. It was however a minute or two before he could find the courage to go to the counter, push through the throng and order a double gin and tonic which he carried to the girl's table where he put it down saying, apologetically,

'You looked so — well — so unhappy,' and at once scurried out of the place as though guilty of a crime. He set off for Toft's place where he had parked his van but to his dismay saw that the girl was following him. He stopped, made a gesture to shoo her away, but she ran until she caught him up.

'Now look!' he said. 'Just because — '

'Don't leave me! For God's sake, don't leave me alone!'

'Look,' he said more quietly. 'You can't come with me. Please go away — go to your home — '

'I've nowhere to go.'

'That's silly! You must have somewhere, so go away!'

But she followed him to his van, and when they reached it got in.

'Now look!' he shouted, but she was staring again as she had in the pub. She was well dressed in a grey suit with white shoes, her slim legs covered with fine silk stockings. Her black handbag looked expensive too. She was obviously not poor but something dreadful must have happened for her to look as pale as a ghost, mouth drooping, eyes staring. He got in beside her, drove through Micklegate Bar, turned off at the race-course where there were fewer people and stopped.

'Now,' he said. 'You must get out, you really must.'

'Take me to where you live. You musn't leave me alone.'

'But I haven't got a place. I live in a caravan.'

'Take me to it.'

When he was nervous Mr Hobart fingered his moustache and he did so now. He had grown it as a disguise for he had reason to believe the police were looking for him. He had often wondered what their description of him would be. They would know he was less than 178cm. tall, aged thirty-five, with dark brown hair and blue eyes, but they wouldn't know about the moustache. But now like a fool he had got himself involved with a member of the public, a thing he had avoided for two years, and members of the public might have been told to be on the look out for him; so it was crazy of him to have got this girl a drink. Hadn't he learned yet that kindness had been his undoing? He said,

'I'm sorry but I can't do that. If you tell me where you live — '

'I had a suitcase,' she said suddenly. 'I must have left it on the train. It'll be in Scotland by now.'

'Scotland! Is that where you live?'

'Where is this place? Is it York? Did I get out at York?'

She was looking at him and he thought the colour of her eyes was blue but the expression in them was so frantic he wasn't sure.

'Oh God!' she cried. 'How could he do it!'

Mr Hobart reluctantly drove on. He was making for the disused aerodrome beyond Bishopsthorpe where he had left his caravan. It was a quarter to one now and he would never get to Norfolk by daylight if he didn't hurry but he drove slowly wondering how he could get out of the mess his foolish gesture had got him into.

'Tell me what's the matter and you'll feel better,' he said.

He wished he hadn't spoken for using those same words had started his own troubles. However, she didn't seem to have heard. Out of the corner of his eyes he saw that she was clasping and unclasping her hands sometimes gripping them so tight the knuckles were as white as her face. He reached the aerodrome where in the shelter of a hangar he had made his camp. His caravan was a second-hand Thompson-Glendale two-berth, as shabby and of the same colour olive green as his van. He stopped beside it, switched off, and said,

'You see? You can't possibly stay here — '

'Please let me stay for a while. Don't leave me alone just yet.'

He unlocked the caravan door. She went in.

'Look!' he said. 'You must understand I'm not the sort of man . . .'

She wasn't listening, staring again, vacant, withdrawn. Mr Hobart had decided not to use any more gas before he got to Norfolk but it occurred to him the girl might be hungry and a meal might bring her to her senses so that she would go away. He lit a ring and put on a frying-pan.

'I've only sausages,' he said.

'What?'

She looked at him as though seeing him for the first time.

'I don't want anything to eat. I'm not hungry.'

But Mr Hobart put two sausages in the pan. If she didn't eat them he would have them cold for his supper.

'I don't get it,' she said. 'To give me the brush-off like that.'

'Yes?'

'I'd gone to his room. I always did. We loved each other, see? But he shouted at me 'Get out!' He shouted. I couldn't believe it. I tried to go in but he pushed me, threw me out and locked the door. He threw me out!'

She put her face in her hands.

'Oh Eric, Eric! Oh God, Eric . . . '

'You just cry,' said Mr Hobart. 'That's the best way.'

He busied himself cooking the sausages, warming the plate by putting it over the pan. He was sure that now she had cried she would go away and leave him alone. The sausages were ready by the time she had stopped crying and was blowing her nose.

'Sorry about that,' she muttered. 'Have you a cigarette?'

He gave her one.

'Could you eat something now do you think?'

She didn't answer but brought her compact from her bag.

'I do look bloody awful,' she said.

He watched her smooth the powder pad about her eyes, take out a little brush, use it on her eyelashes, then shake her head and give up. She put away the compact, took up the cigarette he had given her, he lit it for her and she said,

'I do feel a bit better now. Who are you?'

'My name is Hobart.'

'Mine is Loraine. It must have been you who got me that drink in the pub.'

'Well, yes, as a matter of fact it was, but — '

'It was very kind of you and I'm glad you did because if you hadn't I'd have thrown myself under one of the buses. I'd made up my mind to do it.'

'It would have been a very wicked thing to do.'

'When you've been hurt,' she answered slowly. 'You want to hit back. If you can't hit back you try to do something that will hurt the person who has hurt you.'

'I've had my troubles too,' said Mr Hobart. 'But I'd never kill myself because of them.'

For the second time he wished he'd held his tongue, but she was frowning, evidently thinking again of her own troubles, of that man who, when she had cried, she had called Eric.

'I believe I could eat something after all. I don't think I've eaten today. I'm not sure. I'm not sure of anything now. I just don't understand what has happened. We were going to be married, everything was Go ... I suppose you couldn't give me another drink, could you?'

'Sorry, I don't keep any spirits here.'

He fetched the table from its place in the wardrobe, set it up, put the plate of sausages before her, gave her a knife and fork. But she ate only half a sausage, pushed the plate away.

'Perhaps I'll be able to eat more later.'

She glanced about.

'I've never been in a caravan before.'

'No, well, now you feel better we must think of where you can go — '

'Can't I stay here?'

'No, of course you can't stay here!'

'I don't see why not.'

'Now look! That's silly. A young girl like you and a strange man — '

'You sound a bit old-fashioned.'

'That has nothing to do with it! It's, well — '

'Let me stay. I'm not quite right yet. Please let me stay a little longer. Besides, I've no money. It's in my suitcase, and I've nowhere to go.'

'Then we shall have to find somewhere because you can't possibly stay here. Surely you have friends?'

She was shaking her head.

'Look!' he shouted. 'You must have! Your parents! You must have a family somewhere! Look, you must have!'

'I wish you wouldn't keep saying 'Look'.' Mr Hobart was so astonished at this remark that his mouth stayed wide open as though he was saying another 'Look.' Before he could decide that she had been very rude she said, 'What did you say your name was?'

'Hobart.'

'Your first name — '

'Harry. But — '

'I am beginning to feel better, Harry, but I think I've been clean off my loaf. It was such a shock — are you sorry

11

you befriended me?'

He wanted to tick her off for the way she had criticized his manner of speaking, and to tell her he regretted very much that he had befriended her, but instead he shrugged his shoulders.

'Eric was the assistant manager,' she said, as though he had asked her. 'I was in Reception. We were in love. At least, I thought — give me another cigarette, will you?'

This time he took one for himself too.

'Must I really go, Harry?'

'Well, look — I can't help saying look, it's a habit and it wasn't very polite of you to have told me about it. As for staying here of course you can't, To start with I'm used to being on my own. You get into habits of doing things. Besides, this is a very small caravan — '

'It's got two bunks — '

'Yes well, maybe it has, but surely you know that people of different sexes — '

'I wouldn't let you touch me if you were the last man on earth.'

'No, well, that's not the point.'

'I think I may be able to think a little straighter tomorrow,' she said. 'Please go on helping me a little longer. Let me stay over this night. When you've made love with a man then for no reason that you can see . . . he wouldn't even look at me this morning.'

Her face had clouded over as though she were going to cry again but she drew strongly on her cigarette.

'I do understand Miss — er — Loraine. I'll tell you what I'll do. I'll go back to York and get myself a blanket and sleep in the van.'

'You don't have to sleep in the van — '

'Of course I must sleep in the van!'

He had shouted so made amends by saying quietly, 'I expect you'd like a wash.'

'Yes, I would. Are you going to York now?'

'Yes — '

'How long will you be? I shan't like being alone.'

'I'll try not to be long. Half an hour or so. I'll be as quick as I can.'

'All right.'

'If you want warm water put on a kettle but please don't keep it on too long. Have a good wash and then just sit still.'

'Yes, all right. I'll just sit still.'

'There's a lavatory in the corner,' he whispered as he went out.

He drove fast into York, his mind racing too. When he reached the store where he always bought equipment he didn't buy a blanket but a new sleeping-bag. He knew he couldn't afford it so when he had put it in his van he sat pulling at his moustache talking to the steering-wheel.

'I must be mad. I should never have bought her that drink and now I've bought myself a new sleeping-bag. Stark staring raving mad, that's what I am. It's as though I wanted her to be there but I don't. She might be an adventuress trying to . . . or she may have been planted on me to find out

14

about me, to get me to go back to Kent. Well, I'll get rid of her tomorrow. I won't have her here. I can't.'

He drove back in such a confused state he took the corners as though his caravan were behind him. Although sure he didn't want her around and if she were he would throw her out, at the back of his mind was the hope that she wouldn't turn out to be a phantom that his two years of solitude had caused him to imagine. The aerodrome came in sight, then the hangar, then his caravan. She was still there, sitting on the doorstep.

2

She had put the kettle on again. If she used much more gas he'd have to start his new cylinder before Norfolk and he hadn't planned it that way. He must tell her to be more economical, especially now that he'd bought a new bag. While trying to find the words he carried his old sleeping-bag to the van laying it among the jumble of things there, returned and put the new one on a bunk. She didn't seem to notice. She said,

'I thought you might be the sort of man who likes a cup of tea — '

'Well. yes, I am, but — '

'I used the loo by the way. What do you do about that?'

'It's a special sort. Now you must really . . . '

She wasn't listening. She was staring out of the window giving little shakes to her head as though thinking again of being jilted. He didn't want her to cry again so to distract her he suggested she come with him outside, and he showed her how to raise and lower the stabilizing legs and fix the towing bracket, and she began to take an interest.

'What's that handle for?'

'That's for lowering or bringing up that little wheel.'

'And that upside-down cup-looking object?'

'That fits on to the bracket on the van. The chain is there in case something gives way. It pulls on the brake.'

She looked around the aerodrome with its broken runways and the bits of machinery left to rust.

'Do you always camp in a place like this?'

'Well yes, in this sort of place — '

'Why don't you go to a caravan site?'

'I wouldn't like to have caravans all

around me. I camp by courtesy, sort of, of the Ministry of Defence like here, or the Minstry of Transport where they've straightened roads. There are always bits of the old road to camp on. I know all sorts of places. I've a very good one near Sheffield.'

'I suppose you're rather poor, Harry?'

'Well yes. I haven't much. Well, about nine hundred a year. It doesn't go far but I manage.'

He was growing uneasy under her questioning, thought of running into his caravan and locking himself in and shouting for her to go away, but she walked in before him.

'A wardrobe! I didn't think there'd be a wardrobe in a caravan.'

She examined everything. Over his bunks there were his books. He was afraid she might take one of them down so he said,

'I'll show you how the bunks are made into beds. You have to put the table away first. It folds like this and goes into the wardrobe. Then you slide the back of the bunk down, there — like that. It's quite comfortable.'

She noticed the new sleeping-bag.

'You've bought a new one.'

'Yes, well . . . '

He didn't know how to explain it. She said,

'You're a good chap, Harry. Awfully kind. I'm very grateful.'

'Yes, well I'd better start thinking of what to give you for supper.'

. . . she didn't eat much of the omelette he made. She was looking restless again. He thought of asking her to tell him more about the man who had jilted her but decided it would be best for her to do so when she felt like it. He suggested she go to bed early, get a good night's sleep.

'I shan't be able to sleep.'

He lit the gas mantle. He had also a fluorescent tube in the ceiling powered from the car battery but he used it only after a long run. He left her to get undressed and for twenty minutes strolled about the aerodrome frowning and fingering his moustache regretting all over again that he had, as she put it, befriended her. When he returned to the caravan he knocked.

'May I come in?'

'It's your home,' she said.

She was in the new bag, her clothes folded at the end of the bunk.

'I wish I hadn't forgotten my suitcase. I've a nightdress in it and twenty pounds.'

'We'll do something about that tomorrow. I'm going to turn out the light. I have to be careful not to use too much gas.'

'Must you sleep in the van?'

'Yes.'

'You needn't you know.'

'Of course I must!'

'O.K. please yourself. I hope I shall sleep but I feel bloody awful. If only I could understand *why.*'

'I've got some sleeping pills. Would you like one?'

'It might help'

'They're supposed to be taken with hot milk.'

He regretted lighting the ring again but told himself that tomorrow she'd be gone and he could economize by having cold meals all day. As the milk heated he worked out how many cold meals he would have to have to save the gas he hadn't meant to use. He poured the milk into a cup.

'Here you are. Take two of these. They'll soon send you off.'

'I'll try not to think about it any more.'

'I shan't be far and no one can get in if I let the catch down. Shall I do that?'

'All right.'

He turned out the light and went to the van. When he'd undressed and got into his bag and found the van smelling of oil and the floor hard he was angry that he should be sleeping there instead of being comfortable in his own bunk in his own caravan. He talked to himself about it telling himself it was all very well being kind to people but they shouldn't take advantage of it, and certainly not criticize the way a person spoke. She was a very silly girl and it was her own fault getting herself jilted, sleeping with a man like that.

He woke with a cold in his head and in a very bad temper.

'Good morning, Harry — oh dear! You've got a cold. I knew you shouldn't have slept in that draughty old van.'

'Well, where else did you expect?' he snapped.

She had laid the table and was cooking on all the rings, all of them full on! She brought him a cup of coffee, fried bread and egg.

'Why do you have a moustache, Harry?'

'Why shouldn't I, if I want to?'

'Because it doesn't suit you, that's why.'

'Really! Well, don't imagine I'm going to shave it off on your say so.'

He had a habit of using the lavatory immediately after breakfast but didn't want to do so with her there. He hoped she would go out but she was settling down as though she intended to stay there all morning.

'It's really quite comfortable,' she said. 'It's just like a little house, isn't it?'

He sneezed. After a while she went to the sink. His bowels were rumbling but —

'I'll start the washing-up if you'll bring the things'

'I rather wanted to — you know . . . '

'Use the loo?' she said over her shoulder. 'Go ahead. I'm not stopping you.'

As he didn't move she looked round and laughed.

'You are a funny old-fashioned chap, aren't you?' adding, 'How far do you want me to go?'

She went out and he told himself she was a very silly sort of girl, and very extravagant. All that gas . . . he used the loo, washed, shaved, changed into his jeans and khaki shirt, hanging his suit in the wardrobe. He saw her strolling on one of the broken runways her hair like honey in the morning sunlight . . . cheeky thing, too damn cheeky by half with her personal remarks. The way she'd told him not to say 'Look.' Really, some people!

By the time she came back he'd washed up, (in cold water), put the dishes and crockery away, folded her sleeping-bag, replaced the bunk in its daytime position, made his caravan his own again. She came in, sat down on one of the bunks while he sat on the other.

'I'm sorry you've got a cold, Harry.'

He didn't answer. She tried again.

'Is it expensive living in a caravan?'

'It's obviously cheaper than living in a house.'

'I seem to remember you telling me you had about nine hundred a year — '

'It's nothing to do with you how much I have.'

'But you told me — '

'That was to distract you. You don't look as though you needed distracting now.'

'Harry, don't be unkind to me. Please don't, I am rather shocked still.'

He didn't mean to say it but it came out.

'I can't think why you were so stupid as to sleep with that man. You might have started a baby.'

'You surely can't be so dim that you've never heard of the Pill? Besides, when you're in love you do whatever the other person wants.'

'Well, you shouldn't have.'

'What the hell do you know about it?' she shouted. 'My God, I wish it hadn't had to be you, you fussy little man — '

'There's no need to be rude — '

'You need someone to be rude to you living all by yourself like this. Who are you? What do you do? I want to know — '

'There's nothing to know — '

'Why do you live in a caravan? And keep moving? With private camps all over the place? Are you running away from something?'

'Look, you mind your own business!'

After a long silence she said,

'I'm sorry. You've been good to me, and now you've got a cold. I shouldn't have flown at you like that.'

He hesitated before replying.

'I suppose I have been living rather a self-centred life, and I'm in a bad mood with this cold. Tell me more about Eric. What do you feel about him this morning?'

'I don't know what I feel. I suppose I love him still. You can't fall in and out of love just like that. But what's the use? He doesn't love me.'

'Where did you meet him?'

'I told you didn't I? We worked at the same hotel, the Wyvern in London. We'd been lovers for six months . . . '

'He treated you very badly.'

'I don't think I went to bed after he'd told me to go away. I caught sight of him in the morning but he ignored me, cut me in fact. I wanted to get as far away as possible. I didn't want to be seen by the other staff. I thought of Edinburgh and went to King's Cross — '

'But you got out at York — '

'I hadn't the fare to Edinburgh in my handbag. So I came to York — and forgot my case. I was living in a nightmare. Don't let's talk about it any more please, Harry.'

'All right. But we must think of somewhere you can go — '

'Can't I stay with you a bit longer? I don't feel I could cope being on my own yet — '

'But if you've friends in Edinburgh — ?'

'I haven't. It was just a place a long way away.'

'Then your parents?'

'I haven't been home for three years. My father is dead and my mother — well, we don't get on. I may think of something but I'm still all muddled up. Getting the brush-off like that. It was an awful shock. I wanted to die. Then you got me that drink. Harry, I'm sorry I called you a funny little man — '

'It was fussy you said.'

'I'm sorry for whatever it was I said.

You're a good chap, Harry. Please let me stay a little longer. I'm sure I'll feel better in a day or two.'

A day or two! Oh no!

He went out of the caravan to walk about the aerodrome trying to think out how he could get rid of her, wondering if he ever would get rid of her. He felt feverish, miserable, blamed his cold on the man who had sold him the new sleeping-bag for that man had had a shocking cold. He walked right across the aerodrome and when he got back she came to the door and said,

'If I can't pay you for my keep I have done something towards it. Come in and have a look.'

She had washed the floor, the walls and curtains, put polish on the woodwork.

'The polish was hardly used. I wonder you bothered to buy it. As for the curtains over the cooker they were absolutely filthy. Bit better now isn't it?'

He had nothing to say. She had gathered ground ivy, wood violets and a few primroses and arranged them in a jam jar.

'I suppose you don't like flowers either.'

'They're very nice,' he muttered.

'You don't sound exactly enthusiastic. You're a funny chap, Harry! Seems to me you're kinda lost. But you must be O.K. at heart. You must be.'

Her eyes were steadily on him. He glanced away.

'I think we had better get hitched up and moving on,' he said.

To be on the move had become a habit but he wasn't going to take her to Norfolk. If he did that he might be landed with her for days so, by country lanes, he went west making for his site near Sheffield. He hoped she might want to go into Sheffield, and once there he would 'lose' her and get away from her as fast as he could.

'Why do you take such funny little roads?'

'Because I like them,' he answered through his nose. 'And they're not particularly funny.'

'Don't you ever get lost?'

'Of course I don't get lost!'

He wished she wouldn't talk. People who talked to the driver ought to be chucked out.

'Is it difficult towing a caravan, Harry?'

He didn't answer until he'd driven a mile.

'You get used to it. Towing makes you a better driver. You have to anticipate more. Now please don't talk.'

But after another mile or so she said,

'What's the matter, Harry? Why so silent? Is it your cold?'

'I'm thinking of you and me travelling together like this. It isn't right — '

'Oh, for Pete's sake! I wish you weren't such a fuddy-duddy — how old are you?'

'I'm thirty-five — '

'Then it isn't old enough to be so bloody dark.'

'What's that supposed to mean?'

'Unlit up, non-cool, no swing . . . you

name it, you are it. Where've you been, for God's sake? There's nothing wrong in a man and a woman travelling around together. Good grief, a friend of mine at the Wyvern was all over Greece with her boy friend last year and nobody minded, not even her parents.'

'Well, they should have.'

In stony silence they drove on mile after mile and by noon they were climbing the hills around Sheffield. Tall spruce, silver fir and larch trees were on either side, the rolling hills beyond, above them high white clouds with plenty of blue in between.

'It's beautiful,' she said. 'Are we really so near Sheffield?'

'Yes — why not?'

They descended a slope to a corner and a stone bridge over a rushing beck. There was no sound save for the music of the water. Near the bridge was an opening in the forest big enough to take the vehicles.

When he'd manoeuvred the caravan into position he unhitched, took the wheelbrace and lowered the legs while she watched him. That done, he said,

'I'm going to get some more eggs.'

'I'd like to come with you, Harry. Where do you get them?'

'There's a village — '

'I'll make you an omelette for lunch — would you like that?'

'I noticed you didn't eat much of the one I made last night.'

In silence again they drove towards Langsett. When nearly there she said,

'I'll sleep in the van tonight.'

He thought of suggesting she go into Sheffield and sleep in a hotel but remembered she had no money. As though she had picked out of his head his thoughts about money she said,

'Harry, could you lend me some money? I want to buy a few necessities. I'd like to get something to sleep in for one thing — could you?'

'Well . . . '

'I'll pay you back. I've got money in my suitcase.'

He had only twelve pounds in his

wallet and there were five days to go before April, when his solictor would send him his monthly money to King's Lynn.

'But when will you get your suitcase?'

'We'll go into Sheffield this afternoon. I'll ring up Edinburgh.'

He handed her seven notes but was very uneasy.

'Thank you, Harry. You're a sport, only I wish — '

'You wish I weren't so dark, I suppose,' he said.

Half an hour later back at their camp she put on a saucepan of water.

'What are you doing?'

'I'm going to wash my pants. I'll do some things for you too, if you like.'

'No thanks.'

He went away, walked beside the stream.

'Clueless!' he said savagely. 'Absolutely clueless!'

He sat on a mossy boulder frowning at the fast flowing stream. He threw in bits of grass, watched them being carried away and gradually saw that he was being carried away in a direction he didn't want to go. He'd spent the whole day being unkind to her and it wasn't like him at all. He'd always been known as a kind man . . . but in the end he'd been too kind . . . and now he'd been too kind all over again.

He walked back, saw she'd hung her pants and stockings on a tree. When he was in the caravan he found that there was another saucepan on and she was looking at his books.

'An *English Course for Schools. The Abbey Series of History.* Three volumes of Shakespeare. You've been a school-master, haven't you, Harry?'

He didn't answer. She began to take down Shakespeare's *Comedies*.

'Put that book back!' he shouted, and snatched it from her.

'All right, all right — '

'And what I am or what I do has nothing to do with you!'

'O.K. O.K . . . '

'And I'm sick of your extravagence and rudeness!'

'And I'm sick of your prim little ways with your 'Looks' and your 'wells' — '

'The way I talk has nothing to do with you either!' he yelled at the top of his voice. 'Just because I was sorry for you in that pub you think you can be as rude to me as you like! You haven't the slightest idea how to economize, washing the curtains and now your things without even asking permission. This is my caravan and I don't want to share it with anyone. You call me old-fashioned but I'm not and if having no swing or not being 'lit up' and all the other stupid phases you use means there's nothing wrong in two strangers living together you'd better think again. I don't know what my friends in Norfolk would say — '

'My God! So now it's 'what will the neighbours say', is it? As though it mattered — '

'It does matter, and I bet your friend and her boy made love to one another, it stands to reason . . . '

He was white and so was she.

'All right! I've had enough! I won't stay with you another minute you stupid little man! I'll go get a job in Sheffield and if you won't drive me there I'll walk!'

She ran out of the caravan to collect her garments, he to start the van. She put her wet things in the bag that had contained her briefs and got in beside him. He remembered there was a gas ring on, got out, ran in, and turned it off.

They were entering Sheffield by the Whirlowdale Road when half-way down it he stopped.

'Loraine,' he said. 'I'm sorry. I — it's being so much on my own. I didn't mean — '

She was on the pavement.

'Get lost!' she shouted and walked away.

3

When he got back to his camp, the first thing he did was throw out the flowers she had picked. Then he took down his volume of Shakespeare's *Comedies* with the idea that he would spend the rest of the day getting on with his *Child's Guide to Shakespeare* started before the catastrophe that had sent him on the run. He took out his marker, his snapshot of Johnnie Appleton taken on an outing to the oast houses of the Weald; recalled the night he had woken to find the boy at his bedside.

'What do you want, Johnnie?'

'I wanna go out and smash winders. Lemme stay with you then I won't do that.'

So he had let the boy stay and Johnnie had cried and cried, cried away his hatred of the world . . .

He fell into a brown study remembering those other nights when Johnnie had either been sent to him by the night porter, or had come voluntarily. He clenched his teeth, closed his eyes, murmured 'No, no no!' His life had snapped into two halves, the first when he had been the uncompromising teacher of young thugs, the other . . . he did not want to think of that other half.

He returned the photo to the book and decided to make for Norfolk at once, and he was there by three o'clock the next day. He had one of his best sites near King's Lynn at Castle Rising where the signposts directed traffic to the Hunstanton by-pass. On the old road there were notices saying *No thoroughfare* for that way now ended below the embankment carrying the by-pass. His pitch was half-way between Castle Rising and the new road in a clearing in the wood, and he was encamped by dusk.

With a knife he kept especially sharp for the purpose he peeled potatoes, prepared carrots and onions and put them with the beef he'd bought in a saucepan and leaving the brew to seethe strolled down the disused road. Lights were coming on in the village behind him as he climbed the embankment, and stood watching the busy cars, some with their lights on, some without. He'd driven over a hundred thousand miles and had always avoided being on the road at dusk because of those drivers who refused to turn on their lights until it was almost too dark to see.

At half-past seven he walked back and was approaching his camp when he saw a light in the caravan! But it wasn't possible — she couldn't be there! He ran. There was no light, only the reflection through the trees from a cottage in Castle Rising.

He switched on the ceiling tube, brought out the table, laid his place, and at eight had his supper of boiled beef and vegetables followed by an apple. Sometimes he paused while eating to stare across the table and once he murmured,

'She wasn't well.'

His favourite inn in King's Lynn was *The Bird of Paradise*. The front entrance and the public bar were on Norfolk Street, the back abutted on to the cattle market where there was a side door into a parlour with horse-hair benches, small tables, and an old piano. It was run by Mr Jarman and his wife: these were the friends he'd mentioned to Loraine. He considered them friends because Mr Jarman addressed him as 'Maister' and Mrs Jarman as 'darling', but they didn't know his name although he'd been an off and on regular for two years.

At noon the next day he locked the caravan and drove into the town, parked the van in the little yard near the back door, entered the pub and sat down in the back parlour. Through the passage leading to the public bar he could hear the other customers. He'd never been in the public bar himself preferring to sit in the back room making it a sort of home from home.

His lunch would cost him twenty pence: half a pint of bitter and the sandwich Mrs Jarman would make for him. She made an egg sandwich with the eggs not quite hard boiled, and still warm. He'd told Loraine about them over their supper when she had only toyed with the omelette he'd made.

Mr Jarman came through from the public bar.

'Hullo, maister! Back in these parts again?'

He spoke with the soft Norfolk burr with a lift at the end of the words. He had a long, pale face and weak blue eyes.

'Whar you maikin' fur this time, maister?'

'Nowhere in particular. I'll probably stay around Lynn for a while.'

'Still caravanning?'

'Yes.'

'Haalf a pint?'

'Yes, please.'

Mr Jarman returned to the public

room as his wife came in from the opposite direction. She was a big woman with a big head and a mass of hair. She walked very lightly; Harry was always surprised at the lightness of her step.

'Hullo, darling! Haven't seen you for a long time.'

'I've been spending the winter in my place in Yorkshire, my winter quarters I call it.'

He hesitated.

'I had rather an adventure last week. Rather funny, really. You see there was this girl — '

'Oh yes, darling. Did you want a sandwich today?'

'Please. Egg — '

'Sorry. I've only beef today.'

He didn't try to talk about Loraine again when she brought the sandwich.

He worked on his book all the afternoon filling several pages of the new exercise-book in his neat, italic hand. At seven he ate some of the boiled beef and afterwards drove into

Lynn but didn't go to *The Bird of Paradise*. He left his van in the cattle market and walked to a square called Tuesday Market Place, turned past the Globe Hotel, and to the docks.

There were black clouds scurrying across the three-quarter moon occasionally scattering drops of rain. He turned up his coat collar and watched the rain hit the water, walked slowly along to a lamp, stood staring at the golden reflection in the river . . .

He returned to the cattle market, drove slowly along the Wootton road and reached his camp at half-past nine. When he had switched off the engine he sat looking at his caravan so dark and silent and lonely within the trees.

He stayed at Castle Rising for three weeks going into Hunstanton or Heacham or Holme to get fresh water or gas. He seldom spoke to anyone and this was how he had lived for two years, sometimes pretending he was happy, more often knowing he was miserable. But towards the end of April he was becoming near to knowing that he couldn't go on like this. He was within a few hours of knowing it when he spent the morning of the last Wednesday in April cleaning his caravan and in the afternoon wandered in the wood and picked blue-bells, purple orchids, sweet smelling wild violets and stuck them higgledy-piggledy in the jam jar: when he sat for an hour staring at nothing until had he looked in his mirror he would have seen a face as sad as Loraine's had been.

That evening he was in *The Bird of Paradise* as soon as it opened.

'Hullo, darling! We've not seen you for some time.'

'No, well . . . you remember I started to tell you about an adventure — '

'Did you, darling? What adventure? I don't remember — '

'I started to tell you but you were busy. No, please stay, please listen. It's about this girl, see — '

'What girl, darling?'

'I want to ask your advice.'

She stood looking down at him.

'We were saying only the other night you come in every now and then but we don't know anything about you except that you live in a caravan. Do you live in it all the year round?'

'Nearly all the year — '

'All alone?'

'Yes.'

'Don't you ever have anyone in to cook and clean for you?'

'That's what I want to talk about. You see, it was like this. About a month ago I was in a public house in York and this girl came in. She looked so — well, unhappy I just had to do something about it so I bought her a drink. You see, she'd been jilted.'

'Yes? Go on, darling.'

'I took her to my caravan and I let her sleep there. I slept in the van, of course. It was a man called Eric who'd jilted her. She told me all about it. He'd given her what she called the brush-off. But then we quarrelled — the girl and I, I mean.'

45

'What did you quarrel about?'

'Well, nothing really — '

'But now you're sorry, is that it?'

'Yes. I've not wanted to admit it but I've been sorry ever since. And it isn't true it was nothing we quarrelled over. She called me old-fashioned and funny, no fussy, well both, so I told her I didn't want her in my caravan.'

'Well, darling, it was your caravan. But didn't she do anything to thank you? For giving her a drink and letting her sleep there?'

'Yes, she did, she did . . . '

'Has she gone back to that man now?'

He glanced up.

'Would she do that, do you think?'

'I don't know, darling, but I'm sure I'd have gone off if — what did she do to thank you?'

'She cooked and cleaned — '

'If I'd cooked and cleaned for a fellow that had helped me and then been turned out I'd have left him to get on with it.'

'Yes . . . '

'But now you want her back, is that it?'

'I — I don't know — '

'Are you in love with her, darling?'

'Oh no, nothing like that! Good heavens no!'

'Then why do you want her back?'

He thought about it, his mind struggling to find the answer. He said,

'Well, I'm lonely. She was company. I told her I had friends in Norfolk but I haven't. I haven't any friends anywhere.'

He was looking up at her, his eyes like a child's.

'Then you'd better go and find her again, hadn't you, darling?'

At seven he was standing in Tuesday Market Place where he'd left the van. Lonely, but for a little while he'd not been lonely. Loraine had come into his life like a sparrow flying suddenly into a lighted hall, and then out again into the darkness, but it was he who was out in the dark.

He returned to his camp and knew there had not been one single time when he hadn't hoped that somehow the girl he'd befriended would be there. He looked at his watch. It was a quarter to eight. It was against his planning to leave a camp so late in the day but he was off by eight.

He was going back to Sheffield to try to find her.

4

By 5 a.m. he was asleep at his site near the bridge. At ten he'd breakfasted, washed and shaved, and soon afterwards, dressed in his brown suit, he was ready to go but he didn't start for he was full of doubt. 'Get lost!' she'd shouted so even if he found her it wasn't likely she would want to come with him again. And if he did find her and she did join him it wouldn't be long before she would ask him questions he couldn't answer.

He remembered the snapshot he'd been afraid she'd find and left the van to re-enter the caravan. He took it out, stood with it in his hands trying to make up his mind to tear it up but to destroy it would destroy so much that had given him happiness, and if he couldn't find her or she refused to have anything more to do with him he'd have nothing. He put it in his wallet.

Back in his van he considered the difficulties of locating her. He didn't know her surname, only that she was likely to try to find a post in a hotel. Well, that was something; having come so far there was no point in giving up now. He drove off; half an hour later he left his van in a free parking place on the outskirts of the city and walked on into it. He entered the first hotel he saw. A girl in glasses in Reception said,

'Good morning, sir.'

'Er — well — yes — good morning. Er — the fact is I'm looking for someone. A girl. She's about twenty-four I think — '

'Name?'

'I don't know her full name, only her first one which is Loraine. She'll be somewhere in Sheffield because she said she'd get a job. In a hotel, as a receptionist — '

'We've no one here called Loraine.'

'Oh. Well, I'd better try somewhere else.'

He hurried out feeling the girl's eyes boring into his back as though she thought him queer. He saw another hotel and here a young man in pin-stripe trousers and dark jacket came to the desk. Harry wondered if Eric would look like this. He told the same story.

'Sorry, can't help you I'm afraid.'

He passed by other hotels because he felt more and more foolish asking questions about trying to find a girl. However, he thought he'd try one more and found a big one in the town centre.

'Excuse me asking, but have you by any chance had an application recently from a — a young woman called Loraine?'

'Surname?'

'I don't know it. You see, she used to be a receptionist in a London hotel — '

'What does she look like?'

The girl here looked only about seventeen and had a freshness that gave him confidence.

'Well, she has short, tawny — no, honey-coloured hair, and — '

'Loraine Elliot might answer that description.'

'Yes, I'm sure she would! Is she working here?'

'No. You'll find her at the Victoria over the road.'

'Thank you. Thank you very much.'

'You're welcome,' said the girl smiling as though she was helping in a romance.

In the Victoria he looked around the large office as though expecting to see Loraine. He said to the girl who came forward,

'I'm looking for Loraine Elliot. I was told — '

'Looking for Loraine Elliot? And what might you want with her?'

'Well, you see, she's a friend of mine — '

'Is she now! That's quite a gimmick.'

She stared at him aggressively.

'I don't know what your game is — sir — but I'm Loraine Elliot.'

He gaped, tried to explain, hurried out.

He wandered back the way he had come, knowing he'd set himself a hopeless task. He came to one of the hotels he'd ignored, for a long time couldn't go in but at last decided to have one more try.

'I'm sorry to trouble you but — well — I'm looking for someone. I wonder whether by any chance you have a receptionist here whose first name is Loraine. You see — '

'We did have a girl here called Loraine. Short, straw-coloured hair?'

'Yes, that sounds like her.'

'Loraine Cartwright. She applied about a month ago — '

'That's right!'

'We were short-staffed at the time. She worked in the dining-room. Knew her stuff — '

'Isn't she here now?'

'No. She left last Saturday. She was trained, you see, and told us she wanted to find a place more in her line. No, I don't know where she went.'

For the rest of the morning he wandered about looking at the people hurrying about their business. He had a meal in a cafeteria staring at every table and at the queue buying their meal. In the afternoon he lost himself, couldn't remember where the parking place was. He tramped round and around, not thinking now of Loraine but if he would ever find his van, and didn't find it until nearly five o'clock. He drove back to his camp and on the way he told himself he'd been very silly to waste all that time looking for her. She was a very cheeky, silly sort of girl, anyway.

He considered returning to King's Lynn where he'd tell Mrs Jarman about it, but he went west instead, for some miles following the B6049, then, skirting Buxton and Macclesfield, by quiet lanes reached a camping place not far from a hamlet called Goosetray. He stayed there one night, drove on aimlessly. It rained and like a refrain through his head with the wiper went the words sparrow out, sparrow in, sparrow out, sparrow in, sparrow out . . .

At Alford he took the B5130, his little house creaking and bouncing behind him. He slowly grew aware that the balance of the towing-gear couldn't be right and that the caravan wheels needed the grease-gun. He was looking for a good place to pull up when he heard the rattle of a motor-cycle coming up behind him. He glanced in his mirror and was horribly startled to see that it was a policeman signalling him to stop. The constable drew level.

'Would you mind pulling over, sir?'

'All right.'

'There's a bit of a verge by that lane, sir. Just pull in there, please.'

He thought of driving on fast but that wouldn't be any good. He drew into the verge, sat fingering his moustache. The policeman stopped beside him.

'You are Mr Hobart? Mr Harold Hobart?'

'Yes. Er — anything wrong?'

'I've orders to locate you, that's all I know. Wait here a while, please.'

The policeman turned his bike and roared away. Harry thought again about making a run for it but left the van for the caravan where he did what he planned. He adjusted the towing-gear and, while using the grease-gun, told himself it was a pity that after all this time Mr Appleton had still been determined to prosecute, had now caught up with him.

He wondered how that had come about. It couldn't have been through his driving licence for he had had a new one for a three-year period just before the catastrophe; nor, he thought, through the van for he had bought it second-hand, licensed and insured along with the caravan, and there hadn't been any incident with the police, he had made very sure of that. But it was no good speculating: it had happened.

Sitting on the doorstep, eyes sad, he

ate a sausage with a bridge roll he had bought in Lynn. He looked at the sky. So serene a day after the rain of yesterday. And at the end of it — *prison*? Well, there was one good thing: he hadn't found Loraine. If that constable had found him with her sitting beside him — my God! How awful that would have been . . .

He'd finished his lunch when he heard the motor-bike returning. Following it was a police-car. He braced himself, tense and pale. The cycle stopped, the car stopped, and out of it stepped Loraine.

'This is your brother, miss?'

'Yes. Hullo, Harry! Sorry to have missed you. Thank you, officer. Thanks very much.'

'No trouble, miss. Glad to have been of help. So long now. So long, sir.'

The car and the bike went off.

'And thank you, Harry, for not giving the show away. You see . . . '

She stopped.

'What's the matter? You look — oh

hell! You want to tell them I'm not your sister. Well, I can't blame you. Go on after them and say so.'

'It's not that, Loraine, not that at all. I'm so astonished. I don't understand — '

'I asked them to find you. I had to pretend you were my brother or they wouldn't have bothered — '

'It's not that either! I just don't understand why you've gone to all this trouble.'

'Harry, I oughtn't to have come back. You've every right to send me away after the things I said. I'm sorry for them now. You were so good to me, I wanted to tell you so again before I was half-way down the road. But now there's something else and I guess I need your help all the more. It's an awful bloody nuisance, Harry, but I'm pregnant.'

5

He drove slowly towards the site he had marked on his map. He did not speak because he was thinking about what she had said, what he ought to do about it; occasionally he glanced at her and realized he had never seen her properly before, had never had her in focus. She was pretty, her mouth so small, her eyes so blue . . .

So in silence they reached the site, sheltered by trees and within the loop of a river. She had been waiting for him to tell her he would help her to get an abortion so when he left the van and unhitched she followed him.

'Harry, won't you say something? I want to know — '

'It's all right, Loraine. I'll look after you.'

She wondered what he meant by

that. She didn't want him to look after her in any sense other than lending her some money and 'holding her hand' while she had the operation; but she couldn't baldly come out with it like that. A chap like Harry wouldn't understand. She tried a different approach.

'Harry, you're different somehow. I always saw you as rather a sad little man but you're not so little; and you've nice eyes, did you know? I thought they were blue but they're grey really. I still don't like your moustache though! You don't look so sad any more. You look — '

'More with it, or whatever expression you use today?'

'Perhaps that's it.'

But she still hesitated to tell him what she wanted of him. Whether he was really more 'with it' she doubted; people like Harry were always so shocked at what other people, modern people, knew was right. But she needed him. He must support her because

. . . he broke in upon her thoughts.

'I must go and get some food. Will you stabilize while I'm gone? You remember how to do it?'

'Yes.'

He had to get away from her, had to be alone so that he could savour this extraordinary happening, to express in private his joy that she had come back. He did not wonder about the circumstances, they would have to be considered later, for the moment they were unimportant.

In Tilston he bought milk, eggs, bread, butter, meat, vegetables. The shopkeeper said,

'You look a happy sort of man, sir, if you don't mind me saying so.'

'I don't mind at all for I am!'

He was smiling to himself all the way back. He didn't now think of her as a phantom which might have disappeared. He knew she would be there, his sparrow. But he wiped away his smiles before he entered the caravan to find her lying on his bunk, her shoes

61

and stockings off. She had made a pot of tea; she poured as he made room for himself beside the suitcase on the opposite bunk, sat looking at her bare toes.

'I'm glad you found your case.'

'It had got to Edinburgh and they sent it to Sheffield for me. Harry, when I knew I was preg — '

'How did you know so soon?'

'I'd missed the pip so I went to a doctor, about the oldest practitioner in England I guess! Anyway, he gave me the usual test and the result came through yesterday. Positive — damn it! I'd been taking the oestrogen pill too — I must be a woman in a thousand, or maybe I've been taking too many sleeping tablets. I don't know — all I do know is that now I'm carrying a bloody bastard — until I get rid of it.'

'Get rid of it?'

'You surely don't imagine I'm going to keep it.'

He was staring, open-mouthed.

'If you do, Harry, you've another think coming.'

'Get rid . . . you mustn't talk about your baby like that, Loraine!'

She laughed.

'Really, Harry — '

'It isn't funny, Loraine. It would be a wicked thing to do, to get rid of your baby — '

'Well, well, well! And I suppose you think the father ought to be told and made to marry me?'

'He must be told. He ought to know of his responsibilities — '

'I won't have him know a thing about it. Anyway, he wouldn't care — and whatever you say I'm going to get rid of the bloody thing, and you've got to help me — '

'Is that why you came back? So that I could help you get rid of it?'

'Well, yes. The doctor wouldn't. Doesn't approve — RC, and all that I suppose. But you were kind to me before so I sort of thought you would be again — '

'But would it be kind to help you get an abortion?'

'Oh, for God's sake, Harry! Do get plugged in — not even a socket! Do you think a girl relishes the idea of being an illegitimate mother? All I am asking is that you kind of support me, perhaps lend me some money — '

'Don't ever think of such a thing again — '

'But good grief, an abortion — '

'Is disgusting. Horrible. Your baby has as much right to live as we have.'

'Oh God, here we go again!'

'It's filthy, and unnatural. You mustn't do it. If you do I can't look after you, Loraine. I can't.'

It had cost him dearly to say those words, to run the risk of losing her again. He expected her to explode in fury so he did not look at her but at her toes which he counted as though doubtful she would have the usual number.

There was a long silence while Loraine tried to find the words to tell him he was the stupidest, most old-fashioned ass she had ever had the misfortune to be with, and that she would go as soon as she finished her tea. But in the end having finished one cup she poured herself another. He said,

'Don't let's quarrel, Loraine. I'm glad you thought of me but by now I suppose you know I'm not the right sort of person.'

He smiled rather wanly.

'Too — what was the expression you used? Plugged in?'

She shrugged, looked away from him. He added,

'Is there no one else you could turn to?'

'I did think of writing to Susie. She's one of the girls who was with me in reception. Her people are working-class and so would understand — and know the ropes . . .'

'Why didn't you?'

'I think it was because I'd feel such a fool — me, the go-girl of the set getting herself in the family way — '

'Then what about your mother?'

'You have to be joking! If she knew I was unmarried and preg she'd throw a fit — '

'But surely, Loraine, your own mother — '

'Surely nothing, not with my mother and her lot. She lives on a little housing estate where everyone knows everyone else's business. She's a boss resident, President of the Ladies' Golf Club, plays bridge for the county and all that caper. She's looked up to, see, and thinks a lot about her status, the way that generation always do. I can just see her face when I walk in and say, 'Hullo, Mum, I'm not married but I'm pregnant . . . ' it wouldn't be one fit she'd have but fifty. So you see, Harry, I *must* get rid of it — not that I intend to go home for we don't get on, but there it is. Harry, do try to see things my way, do help me, won't you?'

He ignored the question.

'When is it due?'

'Somewhere around the tenth to fourteenth of December, the doctor thought, but what of it? It doesn't apply.'

She saw he was frowning as he looked out of the window and knew he was mentally far ahead, thinking of December. Poor old Harry! The fuddy-duddy who thought having an abortion was horrible, immoral he probably meant. Well, she would have to persuade him otherwise, make him help her get things sorted out with a hospital, take her to it, look after her a little until . . .

Until what? Until she had got over it? But there was nothing to get over, it was nothing . . . but now she too was staring out of the window, wondering whether the operation hurt, whether she would be all right after it, if she would have regrets . . .

She looked around the caravan, the little home she had known and liked, knew she didn't want to leave it, not yet, anyway. She had better postpone decision on the abortion until — well, until she'd put Harry in a more reasonable frame of mind. Anyway, he must take her to a town for if he wouldn't lend her money she would have to earn it. She said,

'Tell me about yourself, Harry. What have you been doing? I've been working as a waitress — I've got your ten quid, by the way.'

'That's all right, Loraine. I don't need it. I got some money when I was in King's Lynn.'

'Where's that?'

'Norfolk.'

'Have you been all the way to Norfolk, Harry? Then what are you doing in Cheshire?'

He hesitated, murmured,

'I came back to look for you, Miss Cartwright.'

'Well, well, well! So you know my name. And you've been looking for me. Why, Harry?'

'You hadn't quite recovered from — from your shock. And you hadn't any money. I thought you might be in difficulties, so I came back.'

He knew she wanted to know more but he silently counted her toes all over again. He wondered whether the fact that both little ones curled over the next meant that she had worn shoes that were too fashionable.

'You're a good guy, Harry, a real good guy . . .'

She thought she might re-open the subject of the abortion but he suddenly jumped up saying harshly,

'Forget it.'

He knew he was not a good guy but a bad one, and that he hadn't come back because he'd thought she might be in difficulties but because he was lonely. He took the tea-cups to the sink, washed them, said without turning round,

'I'll look after you as I said I would. For as long as you need me. But there'll come the time when you'll need a woman around — '

'Harry, Harry, I've told you — '

'I know what you've told me and I've told you you mustn't do it. So I think you'd best write to your mother — if she hasn't seen you recently she may have changed her mind, grown more tolerant. Where does she live?'

'You do cling to things, don't you?'

She controlled her temper, went on, 'She lives in Leeds.'

'Leeds? Well, that's not far. We could go and see her — '

'The Leeds in Kent.'

'Kent?'

'It's a village not far from Maidstone. When my father was alive he went into Maidstone every day to work, and take me to school there. It's a bigger place now, a dormitory for people working in Maidstone or commuting to London — what's the matter? Don't you like Kent?'

He was thinking that Mr Appleton lived in Kent, the Community Home was in Kent. He was known in Kent. He mumbled,

'It's rather far, that's all.'

He put the washed cups away.

'I don't believe that's the reason. You looked real goosey when I mentioned Kent. Why?'

He put the tea-bags in the trashcan.

'I never go to Kent because you can't get there without encountering an awful lot of traffic — '

'Don't be ridiculous, Harry! You must have driven through oceans of traffic. Either you simply don't like Kent as a county — or is it that Kent doesn't like you?'

He didn't answer because he was thinking that it was a pity this thing had to come between them so soon, that he would have to lie to her so soon. He put the tea-pot away and stood leaning against the sink facing her. She said,

'You looked pretty green when I arrived in that police car . . . are you in trouble, Harry? I'd like to think you were because that would make us even.'

He wanted to deny anything of the sort but he said,

'I shall never tell you, Loraine, so you

may as well not ask.'

But she went on relentlessly,

'I remember something else. Didn't you say when we first met 'I've got my troubles too?' I'm sure you did.'

'It's got nothing to do with you — '

'But good grief, man, anybody would want to know why you don't like the idea of going into Kent. Come on, Harry! You helped me so let me help you. I don't care what you've done — '

'Ask me no questions and never refer to this again.'

He spoke with the firmness and the authority he had had with first the Borstal boys and then those others. The sudden hard tone bewildered and frightened her so that all she could murmur was,

'O.K., O.K . . . '

Slowly the rock-like expression on his face peeled away. He said, as though carrying on a simpler conversation,

'Did you like being a waitress?'

For a moment she couldn't find the words or the breath to say them with.

'It was all right. I made some money. There were many Jews in my hotel and they tipped well. I can give you back —'

'Not now. You can pay for some of the food when next we go shopping.'

Her inquiry was killed stone dead. She had to think of something else to say to bridge the gap, murmured,

'I — I didn't know how I would find you but I remembered the van number and told the — them, a lot of fibs. I told them my name was Hobart and I'd been supposed to meet my brother in Sheffield but had missed him. Could they help? They did — smart of me, wasn't it, Harry?'

'Very.'

He was glad she had used the word brother, for that must be the relation-ship between them. He wondered whether a Hobart with a sister would confuse the chase . . .

He suggested he show her the 'amenities' of his site and took her outside.

The caravan stood beneath trees, chestnuts — candles blooming — oak and ash, and the van by the lane where honeysuckle and briars grew over the hedge of thorn, elderberry, and ivy. From beyond the caravan the river curved in a wide circle, and sang its way under a stone bridge with weed and moss on the supporting pillars. Nearer there were sand banks, shallows, and pebbly shoals — a useful place for washing feet or clothes, he told her — with round a bend upstream bulrushes and deep water. They stood on a sandy spit, the sun on their backs, looking at the rushes.

'It looks swimmable up there — when you're caravaning, Harry, where do you bathe?'

'Most towns have public baths.'

'I think I'd like a bath now.'

'I was in the sea at Holme last week. It wasn't too cold, not for April. Are you really going in, Loraine?'

'Yes. Will you bathe too, Harry?'

'Er — no. I'll peel some spuds.'

'You must let me do the cooking as long as I'm with you.'

'I'd like that.'

She thought of adding that she wouldn't be with him long; she would have the abortion then go back into the hotel business. But she said,

'Come on back to the caravan, Harry, and I'll put on my gear.'

He put the potatoes into the bowl, felt he ought to take them outside but stayed, his back to her, bending over them with his sharp peeling knife.

'Are your ears pinned back? I'm doing a strip-tease!'

She chatted while she undressed and he peeled the potatoes. He listened to her, liking the sound of her voice, hadn't realized how musical it was.

'You can turn round now.'

She was in a red bikini and briefs. He turned away again.

'Every man likes to see a girl in a bikini, Harry, so don't pretend you're an exception — you poor old stick-in-the-mud! I can see that having me around for a while is going to be good for you. Get you out of yourself a bit!'

She put a towel over her shoulders and from the rear window he watched her tripping gingerly over the grass.

'Don't go too far,' he called. 'There may be weeds.'

'Not to worry. I'm a good swimmer.'

He put the potatoes in a saucepan of cold water, added salt. 'Get you out of yourself a bit.' Would that be good for him? He avoided facing an answer by telling himself that he must remember to mention he'd salted the water.

When she returned, hair wet, bikini clinging, he went to the van. He took with him his sleeping-bag, cleared a better pitch for it, further away from his spare battery, tool-kit, grease-gun, petrol cans, trunk, oil drums — all the stuff he'd accumulated — and put sacks on the floor beneath the bag.

For their supper she gave him vegetable soup, Irish stew, apple-tart, and egg custard. It was the best meal he had had for two years and he thanked her for it, resolutely refusing to consider the cost . . . she told him she could do better but looked askance at the stove doubting its ability, not hers.

'You ought to have a radio, Harry. It would keep you up-to-date.'

'As a matter of fact I have one, but it's gone wrong. I meant to have it fixed in York.'

He fished it out from under his bunk. 'What's the matter with it?'

'I'll get it mended for you. We'll take it into Chester tomorrow.'

She wondered whether when they were in Chester, she would leave him as she had in Sheffield, make for a hospital, or apply for a job in a hotel. No, she didn't think she would. Not yet.

She had been looking at his books. Well, it wouldn't matter now if she took any of them down. He said,

'I think I'll go to bed.'

'Must you go to the van, Harry?'

'Yes. I've made myself more comfortable there now.'

'It's the chief thing that made me hesitate about coming back, turning you out of your own place. If you insist on us separating, let me sleep in the van.'

'I wouldn't hear of it. Goodnight.'

The moon was at the full and there were no clouds. It shone through the back window and he undressed by its light, wriggled into the bag, lay with his hands behind his head. When he had last been in circulation, as he thought of it, there had been a lot of trips to the moon and then they'd sent up a sky-lab manned by Russians and Americans — but he hadn't seen a newspaper or listened to a broadcast for . . . he couldn't remember for how long. That had been stupid: his years of solitariness and running away had turned him in upon himself, turned him into somebody he didn't know.

His jeans were hanging over an oil drum. He could see the bulge made in the hip pocket by his wallet. What would she have said if he had truthfully answered her question, told her why he daren't go into Kent, told her about Johnnie . . . ?

He shivered. He could never do that. He would help her, look after her, but tell her about that behaviour with Johnnie Appleton — oh God no, never!

In the caravan, Loraine was also staring at the moon. She was wondering why she was still with Harry and not in Sheffield having her abortion. Nor could she find any sensible answer so telling herself she might as well go along with poor old Harry for another week or two she turned her back on the moon and slept.

6

After their breakfast of scrambled egg she left the caravan for a stroll by the river. It was a tactful gesture, and a little later he did the same.

'You needn't, you know,' she said, but he walked to the river, stood staring into the ripples, threw in some grass, remembered the savage mood he'd been in when last he'd done that; switched his thoughts to that man, Eric, who had seduced her, started her baby. It wasn't right that he should know nothing about it. It wasn't right at all.

When he returned she was lying on her bunk reading one of his exercise-books.

'It's good, this kids' guide and I like your handwriting. Do you hope to get it published?'

'I don't know. I enjoy writing it.'

'You know a lot about Shakespeare,

don't you, Harry? You'll have to educate me.'

He didn't rise to that but said,

'Would you like to come out to lunch?'

He had decided that he must talk about Eric again and considered a meal out might put her in a receptive mood.

'Will you let me pay my share?'

'I'm not so sure about that — '

'No dice then.'

'All right — '

'Then I'll come. It would save quite a lot of gas too, wouldn't it?'

She was pulling his leg. He smiled too.

'Give me a moment.'

The moment was twenty minutes, and when she came out he goggled. She had changed into a smart blue suit with short skirt and jacket, with a white, frilly-fronted blouse and a small, amber-coloured straw hat with red cherries. She had made up her eyes and her lips and she paused in the doorway like a model.

'Will I do?' she asked.

'I'm not surprised Eric fell for you,' he replied.

She gave a snort, thought better of it and said,

'Thank you Harry. Thank you for everything. I've made up my mind never to be rude to you again.'

'That's all right — ' he began.

'It's not all right!' she said. 'You shouldn't be so bloody self-effacing, and when I'm being bitchy . . . '

She caught his comical expression, laughed, and continued meekly,

'Aren't you going to put on your suit?'

'I'll try to match your beauty,' he said.

He was ready in five minutes and they went off, spoke little enjoying the drive along the quiet lanes, the sunshine and dark clouds. There was a shower and he switched on the wiper. Sparrow out, sparrow in, sparrow out, sparrow in . . . sparrow in! He gave a side-long glance at her knees, wanted to tell her of the refrain in his head and why it had come to him but couldn't find the words.

They came to a village. He stopped.

'There's surely nowhere here where we can get a meal?'

'The village pub.'

'But I thought . . . '

He knew she was disappointed; that her thoughts had been of experiencing a little of the life she had known.

'You'll like it here — you will, you know.'

They found the village inn, went into the bar parlour. A Walls' van driver and his mate were sitting at one of the small round tables doing accounts. When they saw Loraine they whistled. Harry wondered if she minded, saw she didn't, and was glad they'd whistled.

'I'll get our drinks and food.'

He knocked on the counter, a man in his shirt sleeves came through.

'What have you got today?'

The licensee chewed, swallowed, and said,

'You caught me just as I'd put in a mouthful! It allus happens! Missus, what we got today? Gentleman in.'

A woman called.

'Beef, and there are some pork pies — '

'Aye, and they'll be oven fresh.'

'What will you have, Loraine? There's beef sandwiches and pork pies — '

'I'll have the lot.'

'Two small pies, two beef sandwiches, and two half-pints of bitter.'

To be saying 'two' instead of 'one' — that was nice. He brought the food to her and she said,

'This is fab! Instead of wasting our dough in a hotel we're going to have a fab. meal at half the cost — how much have you spent, Harry?'

'About seventy — '

'We couldn't have got away with less than two or three quid in most places. We used to charge three at the Wyvern.'

'Which reminds me — what about Eric?'

The barman brought their beer.

Loraine drank, absent-mindedly put her little finger within the rim of the glass and sucked it.

'I've not often had beer,' she said. 'Lager and lime sometimes but not draught bitter. When you work in a hotel you have to be careful about drink. It being all around you you can get the habit and drink too much. I used to ration myself to a glass of sherry and an occasional cocktail, though sometimes the wine-waiter — '

'Are you trying to avoid answering my question?'

'No. I'm thinking about it.'

The Walls' men went away both taking a last look at the lovely girl. Loraine watched them go, glanced all around the little bar, gazed at a faded photograph of a group of men standing with a dart board outside the pub. She said,

'I didn't want to think about Eric any more but now you've asked . . . it isn't easy to say. My experience with him was — what's the word I want, Harry?'

'Traumatic.'

'Could be. I don't know. Anyway. I was so sure of him, so terribly in love with him. I had no doubt whatever that a life of bliss with him was opening up for me. And success. We were going right to the top together. All systems were Go, and I slept with him, was happy to be with him, loved his love-making, loved to make love to him — but you'll not understand that.'

Harry stared into his glass.

'Then suddenly it was all over. No more kisses, not even friendship. I was shattered — well, you know I was, and I can't understand it even now. God, that ghastly dawn when I'd not slept all night. I was so shocked I didn't know what I was doing, not even when I packed my things and fled. I didn't know who I was — but began to know when a kind man brought me a drink.'

Now she looked at him. Harry wiped the froth from his moustache.

'But now, Loraine, today when you know you're having his baby — what do you feel about him now?'

She was silent, first staring at him then, as he had, into her glass.

'I don't know,' she murmured. 'I know he used me rather than loved me but I can't forget him. Is that because I'm carrying his child? And the longer I carry it the more I'll think of him? I suppose that's why — or one of the reasons why — I want to get rid of it. To get Eric out of my system. Does that mean I'm still in love with him?'

Harry was thinking that somewhere in this there was a parallel with himself and Johnnie but he couldn't see it clearly. He said,

'I don't know, but perhaps a woman must always be a little in love with the man who fathers her child. But will you tell him? I do think he ought to know — '

'And be brushed off again? No thanks. But you can tell him if you like.'

'Me?'

'I doubt whether you'll give the thing a rest until you do something about it,

Harry. I wish you would, but you're too bloody obstinate.'

Now was the moment to tell him there was no point in bringing Eric into it as soon there'd be no child for him to be the father of; but she went on,

'Eric was brought up an RC so he may think he ought to do something. Might even think he ought to marry me. I suppose that's the kind of solution that would please you?'

'I'd be glad that the child would have a father.'

'Well anyway, I'm not going to risk another run-along from him.'

'All right. I'll see him. What's his name?'

'Spearman. Eric Spearman.'

'Is he still at the Wyvern?'

'Maybe, maybe not. He'd been there a year before I arrived and assistant managers, especially the ruthless, ambitious sort, try to get a top job. I can find out. I can write to Susie. She'll be there still because she's got a steady boy friend in town. For a while she had a bloke all hair and whiskers, looked like Jesus Christ dressed Carnaby. Until George came along, short back and sides. She adores him — I guess we females all fall for virility in the end.'

He could see that she was thinking of Eric again, which made him think about Eric too, wondering what kind of a man he was, who could seduce and desert a girl like Loraine. And Loraine was thinking on almost exactly the same lines. She said,

'Anyway, Susie threw out the hairy one and went steady with George, the rugby feller. I'll write to her and find out if Eric is still there. Where shall she answer to?'

'Poste restante, Chester. We've got to go there anyway to have the transistor fixed. Ask her to write to you there.'

They found their way to the village post office, bought a letter-card, Loraine scribbled a few words but with misgiving. She said again she didn't want him to know, but Harry took it, and posted it before she could stop him.

Three days later they went into Chester where Loraine had a hot bath and a hair-do while he left the radio to be fixed and walked to the General Post Office where he picked up a registered envelope for himself and a letter for her. They met at a cafeteria for lunch. Loraine read her letter to him.

* * *

'Darling Lorry,

'It was great hearing from you but fancy asking after Eric after the bloody awful way he treated you. The Big White Chief kicked up a frightful stink about it, never having had a girl walk out on him before. He got to know more or less why and had Eric on the carpet. By the way, I found your engagement-ring in your room and gave it back to him with a few choice words. But really, Lorry, you are well out of him, and I shouldn't get in touch with him if I were you but if you really want to know where he is you remember Jackie who came a week or two before you went off? Well, Jackie had a letter from him the other day asking her to join him in a place he'd bought though I bet it was his Pa bought it for him. From the look of the throw-aways he sent her it's a nice place, all rural-like, catering for anglers and such, and it's called the Armstrong Hotel, Grassingdale Ridge, Yorks. It wouldn't suit me and it won't suit Jackie but she's going so now you know why he threw you over. She's just about right for him with the manners and figure of a barmaid all through her fat self. If she sticks to him she'll have the place off him one day and serve him right, the sod.

'I just can't think why you want to have anything more to do with him but I've always said we girls go crazy sometimes. I was crazy for Jesus, wasn't I? Anyway, that's where you'll find him but if you take my advice you'll forget the so-and-so.

'Are you going to work in Chester? All the best if you land a job there. The *Queen* isn't bad — it was O.K. when I was with them.

'Love,

'Susie.'

Loraine flipped the letter across the table for Harry to put in his pocket.

'I should have guessed — how stupid can you get?'

'This other girl you mean?'

'Who else? She must have been with him that very night — and she'd been sweet as syrup to me all day . . . '

'She may not like to hear he's got someone — you — in trouble — '

'If it was anyone but you, Harry, I'd say you have to me joking. 'Might not like!' Jackie wouldn't give a damn if he had fifty illegits knocking around — '

'Then she ought to care.'

There were sparks in her purple eyes and her mouth was no longer pretty as she said,

'You're a laugh, Harry, just a great big laugh.'

'All right. I'm a laugh. But he's got to be told.'

'Look, Harry,' she said biting her lips to keep back ruder words. 'I loved that feller and slept with him expecting to spend the rest of my life with him. But he walked out on me. Now it doesn't matter if I love him or don't love him. It's finished.'

'I don't see it like that. I see a man who is going to be a father — '

'You!' she exploded. 'The most stupid, grooveless idiot it could be any girl's misfortune to meet! My God, what a ghastly goof you are! Bloody little man! Can't you see I'm right about getting an abortion — '

'That has nothing whatever to do with it,' he said, stopping her in mid storm. 'Your baby has rights of its own. I told you. As for its father, if he says he won't do anything about it, all right, but I shall know he knows. And I shall see that he does something about maintenance. You'll need that later on.'

It seemed as though she would throw the plate she held but he was looking at her as he had when she had questioned him about Kent: and as he had looked long ago when a Borstal boy had picked up a chair to hit him with. The chair was put down and so was the plate.

'O.K.,' she muttered. 'Have it your way — but I'm not taking him to court to expose the whole bloody mess, that's final. When will you go?

'I shall go tomorrow. I can do it in a day if I start early enough.'

And at six o'clock the next morning he was off.

7

He disliked the journey. Most of it was through built-up areas, row upon row of ugly stone terrace houses. There was an air of poverty over this part of England between Lancashire and Yorkshire which made him feel sorry for the people who lived here.

But there were other reasons for his depression, and one became so strong that at Hebden Bridge where he had his lunch he ate little, and after it, sat in his van asking himself what he thought he was doing.

Never a man able to analyse himself he was at a loss to know why he'd undertaken this task. When with Loraine it had seemed the right thing to do; now he was full of doubt. He realized that in a backhand sort of way she had inspired him, had given him the confidence he used to have; but now that she wasn't with him he was wondering whether his kindness was again leading him into an impossible situation?

He resumed his journey but the nearer he drew to Grassingdale Ridge the gloomier he became. By half-past two he was on the high moor whose beauty did not register he was so preoccupied, and just before the hamlet he stopped, sat for nearly twenty minutes thinking of turning back. He was reasoning now that Loraine's affairs were not his; she had made a fool of herself with a man; it was nothing to do with him, and by making it his affair wasn't he letting himself in for all sorts of complications? If he failed to induce this man to marry her, to 'give the child a father', he would have her with him until the child was born and he couldn't afford it, not only in the money sense: in the course of time she was sure to ask him those questions he dreaded. He'd shut her up once but . . .

He took out his wallet, looked into it as though afraid that by some misfortune he'd left that snapshot behind, but it was still there.

And if he succeeded, perhaps even brought the man back with him, what then? He would lose her again, would go on living, existing rather, as he had done for so long, alone.

He couldn't decide which of his dilemmas was the worse so at length told himself that since he'd come so far he may as well see this chap. At three o'clock he was parking in the drive of the Armstrong Hotel. He walked in. A young man rose from a chair in the corner of the reception office.

'Good afternoon, sir.'

'Er . . . good afternoon.'

The man was of about his own height with sleek fair hair, a pointed nose, and prominent blue eyes.

'Are you looking for accommodation? If so, I'm afraid — '

'No, not accommodation. I'm looking for someone.'

'Yes?'

'I am wondering whether a Mr Spearman is in?'

'I am Mr Spearman.'

'Not — not Eric Spearman?'

'Yes. Why the 'not'?'

'Oh. Could we go somewhere private?'

The young man put his hands on the counter.

'I don't think so,' he said after a prolonged stare. 'If I may say so — sir — you look a little as though you might not be up to any good — '

'Oh no. No, really. Quite the contrary. I am trying to be up to some good.'

'All right. What do you want?'

'It's about Loraine. Are you going to marry her?'

He hadn't meant to start like this at all.

'Are you talking about Loraine Cartright?'

'Yes, of course. You see — '

'Are you a relation? Brother? Or something?'

'No. No relation. Just a friend.'

'Just a friend, eh?'

The way he said it, the steady stare, made Harry angry.

'It's not that at all! She's going to have your baby, Mr Spearman, so I think you ought to marry her.'

There was a short silence during which those eyes seemed to bulge a little more. A smile playing about his thin lips the man said,

'Not by me, she isn't, mate.'

It was five seconds before Harry closed his mouth.

'Not?'

'Not.'

'But — but she told me — '

'What did she tell you?'

'Why — why that you asked her to marry you, that in fact you were engaged. You made love to her and now she's having your baby — '

'And you believed that?'

'Of course!'

'Why 'of course', mate? Loraine's quite a nice kid if you like 'em that way.

I don't. I prefer 'em less prickly. And for another I never asked her to marry me and I'm not going to get myself mixed up in her mistakes, see?'

Harry didn't know whether he did see or didn't.

'I know what Loraine told me — '

'So you come beetling along, a knight in shining armour and all that jazz, to slay the dragon — oh no, you were asking him to have a bastard foisted on him. Well, mate, you've got another think coming. Her brat has nothing to do with me — so you'd best get out before I ring for a porter.'

'But ... I must know the truth! Loraine wouldn't have told me lies. I can understand you not wanting to marry her on — just on my information, but — '

'I said out — sir — or do I have to get a porter to throw you out?'

Harry went to his van, drove a little way, stopped. He was completely confused. 'Not by me she isn't, mate. Her brat has nothing to do with me'.

In his mirror he saw Mr Spearman crossing the road. He had a flat cap and walking-stick and was going through a gate on to a footpath. Harry wondered where he was going, remembered the barmaid Susie had mentioned, thought perhaps he was going to meet her. He left the van and followed, catching him up near a stile.

'Hey you!' he shouted.

Mr Spearman turned round.

'I told you to get out.'

'You called Loraine a liar!'

'I didn't, but she is — '

'It's you who are the liar! Loraine wouldn't have lied to me!'

'Go away!'

The young man raised his stick, Harry rushed forward, seized the stick, wrenched it away.

'I'll teach you to call her a liar, you filthy little beast!'

Mr Spearman turned and ran. Harry rushed after him, beat him across the back, beat him again and again as he lay over the stile. He could have killed him, but the man got over the stile and fled. Harry threw the stick after him.

He was half way to Preston before his blood cooled. He pulled into a lay-by and there stayed ill-at-ease for a quarter of an hour.

He shouldn't have done that. Eric might have been speaking the truth. He could bring an action for assault. It'd be in all the papers . . .

'Not by me she isn't mate'.

Was it Loraine who was the liar? But why? If her story was a pack of lies, why had she come back to him?

His imagination ran riot. She wasn't having a baby at all; she was a police-woman! Or had Appleton planted her with him, to lure him back into Kent? Or perhaps she was an actress, out of work getting her food and shelter by a trick . . .

At half-past ten he was going down the lane to his camp, his mood as black as the night. By now she was a thief, and had stolen his caravan — but it was still there faintly showing in the starlight. It would be empty, his May money gone . . . but as he switched off the engine a light appeared behind the green curtains, then the door opened and she called.

'Harry?'

'Yes.'

'Thank goodness! I've hated being here alone all day, and when it grew dark there were owls hooting. I'm sure one was on the roof. Then some boys came by and banged on the sides until I shouted at them to go away. Come in. You must be tired out and hungry. How did it go?'

He sat on a bunk staring at his hands.

'Perhaps you'd like to eat first? I've made you some egg sandwiches and coffee . . . what's the matter, Harry? You look dreadful — what happened?'

'He told me the baby had nothing to do with him.'

She sat beside him.

'And you believed that?'

'I don't know what to believe! Tell me it isn't true, Loraine, that you haven't been telling me lies?'

She took his hand.

'No, Harry, you silly boy, I haven't been telling you any lies. All the same, I'm a fool to have let you go. A man, no man and certainly not a man as sophisticated as Eric, is going to admit paternity. How could he? And to a stranger? He probably thought you were my lawyer.'

'You did sleep with him? You are having a baby? You've not been deceiving me?'

'All I told you is true, Harry, but whether you believe it or not is up to you. You'll have to use your own judgement. But all I can say is that I've never told you any lies, and I never will.'

She saw the tears in his eyes before he could turn his head away. He went out, walked by the river. After a while he washed his face in the cold water and came back, did not look at her as he sat down.

'I'm a fool,' he said.

'Would you like some supper now?'

She brought the sandwiches and coffee.

'I must say I think you are, considering Susie's letter. How far did your doubts about me go?'

'I'd rather not say!'

'O.K.! Anyway, we're quits on the crying caper, and I can't be sorry about that. I can be bloody bitchy and think I'm neon lights all the time, but I don't mean the half of it, Harry, you must know that by now. And I'm glad you saw him for now I can see him as I ought to see him, as the filthy little — I'd like to use a four-letter word that alliterates with filthy — '

'I called him filthy, Loraine. And I beat him.'

'You what!'

'I beat him. With his own stick. He ran away.'

She laughed and laughed.

'Well done, Harry! I could kiss you for doing it!'

He looked so startled she covered his

embarrassment by saying with a yawn,

'I'm tired. It's a nervous tiredness I guess. I hated being alone — '

'I'm tired too. I'll go to the van — '

'Oh no you won't. I'm not going to be left alone any longer. I'll go get your sleeping-bag.'

She was out before he could move, in before he could make up his mind what he ought to do.

As he hesitated with his braces off she said,

'I reckon we're using too much gas, don't you?'

They undressed in the dark and soon he was in his sleeping-bag across from her. He felt her presence, wondered about being so close to her, thought about it for a long time. He wanted to say something about it, not sure what. He wondered if she were still awake, whispered,

'Loraine?'

But she was asleep.

8

He woke early, looked across at her still asleep. Her short hair reminded him of Johnnie. He left his bunk angry with himself for thinking of Johnnie, put on a kettle. The tea ready and Loraine awake he gave her a cup, sat on his bunk drinking his.

'I've something to tell you, Harry,' she said. 'I've decided against an abortion — no, don't ask me why because I don't know why. I'm going to keep the baby, that's all. I made up my mind some time yesterday.'

He was pleased but said nothing.

A few days later she began to suffer from morning sickness. He woke to hear her vomiting into the sink. On the third morning she suggested he go back to the van for, as she put it, waking up to hear someone being sick was no bloody joy. He demurred but she insisted and he knew she would be happier alone for the present.

He had liked being with her, missed her nearness and their bedtime chat. But the notion that he might be in love with her couldn't enter his head because of that Thing binding him down like Pilgrim's burden. Besides, had she not said they were brother and sister? That must always be the relationship between them. *Always*.

She said to him one day,

'I get the bloody shakes at the thought of giving birth, Harry.'

'I can understand that. It makes me more sure than ever that one day we must tell your mother.'

'Not that again, for God's sake! It'll be the same fiasco you had with Eric. She'd reject the whole thing as something that couldn't happen in *her* family. Even if she *saw* it was true.'

'What do you mean, saw?'

'Women grow big when they're having babies, didn't you know? In another four months I'll be as big as a drum, so we'll show her then, shall we? Is that what you want?'

She wondered what he would say with his phobia about Kent, then suddenly out of nowhere came the wish that things were different between them, that she was not having a baby by another man, that she had never gone with that man. She almost recognized the wish that she was in a position to love this man, but with a kind of inner screech of horror she suppressed it. Good grief! Not that! Not Harry!

'I said we'll think about it,' he was saying. 'Didn't you hear?'

'Oh. Did you?'

'Yes. What were you thinking about? Or were you feeling sick again?'

'Yes, I was feeling sick. Mortal sick . . . let's move on somewhere, Harry.'

'Where would you like to go?'

'Let's go somewhere where I can have a swim while I still have my figure. On the coast, Harry — let's go now!'

'All right. We'll make for Norfolk. I'll go get the radio while you pack up

— you know what to do?'

'Yes, I know what to do.'

He was back from Chester by ten when he buried their rubbish, filled in holes; and were in Newark by half-past one where he took her into the *Clinton Arms*.

'I'm sure we can't afford a lunch here — '

'Apart from I hope stirring up your appetite, I've a reason for having a good lunch. Tomorrow I shall be thirty-six, so I am giving myself a birthday party.'

'I must go shares — '

'No.'

'All right then I must buy you a present.'

'O.K. I'd like that.'

After lunch — roast duck — they sat in the glass covered lounge.

'There used to be a parrot — died of old age I guess.'

'It was my birthday when I was in Sheffield. I'm twenty-four now.'

Their coffee arrived. As he watched her pouring it he thought of Eric. She had expected to be married to him, pouring out coffee for him . . . what on earth could she have seen in that man? That miserable little pip-squeak . . .

'You're looking very tense all of a sudden. Give.'

'I was thinking about Eric. I was wondering what you saw in him.'

She let out a stream of cigarette smoke.

'A man hasn't got to be handsome to attract a woman if he has virility. Eric had that. And he was modern, by which I mean there was nothing soft about him anywhere. He had that hard up-to-the-minute swinging outlook which I thought important.'

'Do you still think it important?'

'I don't know. I'm not so interested in the modern scene now, being out of it.'

He wondered if she liked being out of it. He said, hoping she would deny it,

'You miss it, though?'

'Sure I miss it, or a lot of things in it. I miss having a natter with the girls about hair-styles, clothes, and men. I miss the telephone and still often imagine I hear it ringing. I miss shops and buying things, going to dances, discotheques, plays, telly. I miss having a proper bedroom with space to be untidy in, and I miss stairs! I'd like to be able to run up and down stairs ... but what the hell! I've an eight-week foetus in me, or maybe it's an embryo, I don't know, and that's enough for me to be getting on with.'

She wouldn't let him come with her into the shop where she bought him her present, nor let him have the parcel which she kept on her knee as they drove on.

'Were you born in Norfolk, Harry?'

'No.'

'Where then?'

She wanted to know about this chap, but he said,

'Does it matter? I don't ask you about your background.'

'I was born in London,' she said. 'In Chelsea. My father was a solicitor working with a firm in Lincoln's Inn Fields. Something went wrong and the firm crashed, and my father joined a firm with a practice in Maidstone. I don't think my father ever recovered from what happened in London. He was often ill. He died when I was fifteen . . . we had very few relatives so hardly anyone came to the funeral. My mother went through the motions of grief but she didn't fool me. Now she could enjoy her golf and her bridge without encumbrance. I went back to school for one more term then she said she couldn't afford the fees, but she could spend oceans of money on her golf, and her bridge parties. However, my O-levels were enough to get me a job and I started in a guest house when I was sixteen, then applied to Trust Houses for training, and so started in the hotel lark. Now, Harry, it's your turn — give!'

'Norfolk,' he said. 'Is the finest county in England.'

He thought she was going to swing

her bag into his face.

'Oh you are a bloody fool!' she said.

By five o'clock they were going along a narrow lane with gentle undulations.

'Here we are.'

He turned through a gate into a two-by-four field, a wasteland full of thistles. It was circular bounded by a thorn hedge as though to keep it from straying, with a gap for a cart up the slope behind it, and an oak growing out of the hedge on one side, a stream near the other.

'Oh no!' she said. 'Not this, Harry!'

'She always looks a bit dowdy when I arrive. I'll soon improve her appearance.'

He watched her swearing beneath her breath as she stalked off towards the stream. He brought a billhook from the van and a rake and attacked the thistles raking them down towards the lane where later he would burn them. Occasionally he glanced at her where she sat on a boulder her hands in the water.

'Can we drink this?'

'Yes. The water comes from a spring at the top of the field. It's very good. The farmer lets me have this site for one pound fifty a week which is pretty cheap these days. I buy my eggs, milk and vegetables from him — I'm ready to stabilize, will you help me?'

She came, helped him, and said,

'How far from the sea are we?'

'About two miles.'

'Well that's some consolation I suppose.'

He manoeuvred the caravan into a good position and she took the wheelbrace while he parked the van near the opening into the field.

'I'd better change into my jeans — '

'Then I'll give you your birthday present.'

She was ready before he was in green slacks and yellow shirt. He jumped from the back of the van grinning. She had bought him a multi-coloured nylon shirt and dark green jeans.

'Like it?'

'Fab! Thank you very much. I haven't had anything new to wear in ages! How do I look?'

'You look something like it for a change.'

She went into the caravan to prepare their supper and managed a goulash with all sorts of odds and ends and all the vegetables they had. He told her it was jolly good but she was in a mood to want more than compliments on her cooking. She said,

'I wonder whether you'll ever stop keeping me at arm's length. Will you, Harry?'

He wondered about that himself, smoked in silence for a while then looked at her as steadily as she was looking at him.

'Yes. I think I will one day.'

'Then give — now.'

But he shook his head, put a match to the gas mantle and said,

'I'll fix the ceiling light tomorrow. The nearest depot for gas is at Heacham about three miles away.'

She had a hair brush in her hand and it looked as though she would throw it at him but instead she began to brush her hair. He stood beside her.

'Why do you have your hair so short?'

'I don't think I could give you a reason. I had it cut when I was twenty-one. I expect I thought I'd look dead glamorous. You'd like me to have it to my waist, I suppose? Dead feminine, eh?'

'Yes, I would, indeed I would.'

He didn't want her looking like a boy.

'O.K. I'll make a bargain with you. I'll let my hair grow if you shave off your moustache. What about that?'

'Why do you want me to do that?'

'I told you. It doesn't suit you. It makes you look forty-six instead of thirty-six.'

He thought about it, wondered if he dared, said,

'All right. It's a bargain!'

The next morning they went to the beach at Holme. They undressed beside a derelict boat, putting their clothes where the tiller had been. She wore her red bikini, he blue trunks. She had imagined he would be skinny but he wasn't. He had a firm, muscular body with fine hairs on his chest, strong arms and legs. Eric's body had been as smooth as a pansy.

As they walked over the ribbed sea sand to the ebbtide edge she asked,

'Am I showing?'

'No — well, I'm not sure. I don't think so.'

'Seven more bloody months, then what? How am I going to take up my career with a kid around, devil damn it!'

He ran into the sea and she watched him swim far out. She didn't go with him because she was afraid a long swim might harm the baby.

At noon they were by the broken boat, she lying on her back, he sitting up looking around. There were more people on the beach than when last he'd been here; more children with their buckets and spades, their fathers with their trouser legs rolled up 'helping', the mothers sitting near-by knitting. There were more young men and their girls entwined together. Harry was watching one couple who hadn't had their mouths apart since he'd sat down. Loraine said,

'Seven more bloody months. Can you put up with me for seven more months, Harry?'

'Yes.'

'Just yes? I sometimes think you don't like me one little bit.'

'Of course I like you, Loraine.'

He glanced at her, suddenly jumped up and she had a close-up of his legs with the hairs like little spiders going up to his groin.

'Where are you going?'

'I'm going for a run.'

He was running away from her because he too wanted to put his lips to a girl for minutes on end. The warm sun, the other couples, the near nakedness of her — it was these that had stirred him so acutely. So he ran, his feet pounding the soft sand, ran and ran until he was half a mile away.

He slowed down, walked in a shallow inlet cooling his feet, took a cool look at himself, murmured,

'You're a b.f. Harry! As though she would ever want you to anyway . . . '

He thought about her baby. Would a man mind starting married life with someone else's baby? If the impossible happened and it ever came to such a thing between them, would he?

'I wouldn't give a damn!' he said and a small boy shrimping looked up at him. 'Well, I wouldn't!' Harry told him. The boy put a finger to his head and screwed it, his way of showing that he considered the man bonkers.

He ran back. She was sitting up now. When he reached her, in one hand she held an ice-cream, in the other Johnnie's photograph.

'Who is this, Harry?'

He was silent.

'I wanted an ice-cream. A man came

by. I pinched a note from your wallet and this fell out. I didn't mean to pry — '

'That's all right.'

She held the snapshot to him, he took it, didn't look at it.

'Son or something?'

He smiled, shook his head.

'Just a boy I used to know. I can't think why I kept it.'

'Perhaps you were fond of him?' she said.

'Perhaps. Anyway, I don't want it now.'

There was a litter bin not far away. He tore the snapshot up, dropped the pieces in the bin, and came back.

'Well?' she said.

He sat down beside her.

'What have you been thinking about while I've been running?'

He could see that she was annoyed but he waited, silent. He had torn up his past — wasn't that enough, even if she didn't know why he'd done it?

'I've been thinking about my baby

— and I don't mean you, you great goof!'

'I've been thinking about your baby too,' he said.

'I could hit you sometimes, Harry.'

'Have a cigarette instead.'

She took one and smoked it as though intending to finish the cigarette, or him, in two puffs. 'And what did you think about your baby?' he asked.

'I wondered whether it would spoil my chances, that's what I was thinking. And now I've decided it won't, see? I shall buy myself a Woolworth's wedding-ring, call myself Mrs What-is-it, and put the kid in a crêche. I'll do that in some town where I take up my career again. What do you think of that?'

'Sounds all right,' he said.

The cigarette had been smoked with such ferocity it was already done. She ground it out in the sand.

'Right!' she said. 'Thanks for the advice. That's what I'll do, then. I'll go to Oxford. To the Randolph. I was in the kitchen there one time. They'll remember me there.'

She was glaring at him but he was looking out to sea.

'I stayed at the Randolph once.'

'So?'

'I stayed there when I went up to take my M.A.'

'We begin to learn something about you after all, do we? Wonders will never cease! You were at Oxford then?'

'Yes. While I was in the hotel I saw some of the page-boys putting what looked like a dog's 'business' on the floor of the reception office — '

She was so angry with him she didn't want to laugh but had to.

'And what happened?'

'They saw I'd noticed, and put the thing back in their pocket. I'm afraid I spoilt their fun. Perhaps they tried again when I'd left!'

He was almost ready to tell her how some of the boys at the approved school had found a joke shop in Maidstone and put stink bombs in the chapel but, if he did, she would guess that the photograph had been of one of them and might begin to guess other things as well. He said,

'And when you have restarted your career, what then?'

'I'll hook on to some up and coming young man in the business and he and I will go right to the top.'

There was a challenging tone in her voice. He murmured,

'That's the career you planned with Eric, I suppose.'

Her hands were clutching at the sand. He expected her to bombard him with it.

'Yes, damn your bloody eyes! It was.'

He laughed. The great big bloody crap had the nerve to laugh at her! She had twice seen in his face an expression of diamond strength but this laughter that now lit up his face, she'd never seen that before.

'You're very merry at my expense — what the hell are you laughing at?'

'I couldn't tell you exactly. Not at

you, Loraine — I feel merry, so I laugh
. . . I am also beginning to feel hungry.
Shall we go home?'

'O.K. you strange, beastly man!'

She was still angry when they
reached the caravan but cooking the
fish he'd bought lightened her mood,
and over their fish and chips she asked
him what interesting places Norfolk
had to offer.

'Burnham Thorpe where Nelson was
born, the Queen's house at Sandringham — and lots of other things. But
this evening we are going into King's
Lynn to meet my friends.'

They were in *The Bird of Paradise* at
seven o'clock. They'd had supper in a
self-service, and bought some stores,
Loraine insisting on getting a bottle of
sherry not so much for drinking as for
using to make her food more agreeable.
Now she sat with her full shopping bag
beside her looking around the little
back saloon bar.

'I used to come here quite a lot,' he
said.

'To meet your friends?'

He was silent, regretting that he'd told her he had friends in King's Lynn when all he had were acquaintances. Mrs Jarman came through from the kitchen.

'Good evening!' said Harry. 'This is Miss Cartright — '

'How de do, my dear. Excuse me,' and she went on through to the front of the house.

'I told her about you — '

'She doesn't seem all that interested — is she one of your Norfolk friends, Harry?'

'Yes. She didn't recognize me.'

He'd shaved off his moustache that morning which is why, he supposed, he hadn't been recognized. Loraine hadn't noticed — well, he'd close clipped it recently which may have been the reason. She'd have noticed all right if he'd kissed her . . . he turned directly to her to tell her about it but at that moment Mr Jarman came in for the order.

'Evening, maister. What would you like, miss?'

'I'll have a bitter, please.'

'Half a pint for both of us, please Mr Jarman.'

'Still got your caravan, maister?'

'Oh yes.'

He went away to draw the beer and his wife returned.

'I didn't recognize you, darling! You've shaved off your moustache!'

Loraine swung round.

'So you have! Well, well, well!'

'I think you look nicer without it, darling. And younger.'

'I thought there was something missing . . . O.K. Harry! I'll trip over my hair as soon as I can!'

'And I think you'd look nicer too, miss, if you don't mind me saying so with long hair. Do you want anything to eat?'

'Mr Hobart was telling me you had a special way of doing egg sandwiches —'

'It's the usual way, darling — at least, I've always done them that way.'

Towards eight Loraine asked Mrs Jarman if she could go and spend a penny.

'Come along with me, my dear.'

Left to himself Harry remembered how often he'd been in this parlour sitting in silence and self-absorbed. He was a different person now, or perhaps he was a former person, the man he'd once been.

'Not quite yet,' he murmured. 'But nearly . . . '

He thought of Johnnie's photo in bits in the litter bin and gave a sigh. It was a sigh of relief as Pilgrim might have given when he'd shed his burden.

Loraine came back and they set off for their camping-place. Harry said,

'I'm happy you've had one thing you said you were missing — '

'What was that?'

'A natter with a woman — well, a bit of a natter, anyway.'

'She's a nice person, your Mrs Jarman. A real, nice person.'

'What did you talk about?'

'Babies. I told her I was having one so we talked about that, and her family too.'

'Anything else?'

She hesitated.

'We talked about you.'

'So?'

'She said that when you used to come in she thought you were like a little boy who didn't know where he was, who'd lost his way.'

'A good description.'

'And always so lonely.'

'True.'

'And trying so hard to pretend he wasn't.'

'I was like that.'

'She said it was I who must have made all the difference.'

'All very true still.'

'And then she asked me if you were in love with me.'

He'd been driving on his side-lights. Now he switched on the headlamps.

'Did she say that?'

'She did. I told her there was nothing

like that between us.'

'And what did she say to that?'

'She said it wouldn't come between us, darling.'

He drove in silence, eyes on the road.

'Nor it should,' he said suddenly, and now it was she who was silent.

'Anything else?'

'I told her you weren't the father, of course.'

'Of course.'

After a minute or two he went on,

'I'm glad you had a talk with her. You must see more of her. We'll go into Lynn for all our shopping. And you must see a doctor — '

'Why? I don't need a doctor!'

'You must be seen sometime, Loraine. As a precaution as the baby grows . . .'

. . . she couldn't sleep for discomfort so at midnight she took her torch — his birthday present to her — the radio and some biscuits and in her dressing-gown left the caravan.

It was warm. There was no moon but the stars shone bright, twinkling in the stream as well. The water rippled and sang so softly over the pebbles reminding her of a poem she'd learned at school. She walked to the boulder she'd sat on before, turned the radio low, ate biscuits and listened to pop.

Was Harry in love with her? She didn't think Mrs Jarman really thought so . . . but he was a funny fellow. A better fellow than Eric . . . better? A thousand, million times better . . .

She slipped out of her clothes, stood naked, felt her breasts and her belly, wondered what Harry would do if he should see her now . . .

He wouldn't do a thing, not a bloody thing! He would pretend she was fully clothed and go off for a trot as he had on the beach. He was a crap . . .

She dressed, turned off the radio, walked towards the van, paused there her hand on the door handle, moved away and hurried back to her bed to which she said,

'He's a crap, nothing but a great big bloody crap!'

9

A month after the event Harry knew for sure that the tearing up of Johnnie's photo had been a release. At the time, he'd burst into merry laughter because by that gesture he knew he'd torn up a silliness he could never repeat: circumstances and his own emotional frustration had caused him to respond to the love of a boy, but now he was himself again, his affections turned towards an object to which they could cling through natural need.

But he could not speak of it, not only from shame but because like a Damoclesian sword a conviction for his behaviour hung over him. And yet in his van alone at night he knew that one day he must tell Loraine what sort of a man (although for so short a time) he'd been and gradually he came to put a term on his confession: after her baby had been born.

June went by with all its splendid sunshine and now it was July and their life had fallen into a simple pattern, the pattern of a married couple though neither thought of it that way, Loraine because she felt too foul to think of anything but release from discomfort.

On the first Sunday of the month Harry came to the caravan in his brown suit to find Loraine lying on her bunk her stomach beginning to show that soon it would be 'as big as a drum'.

'So you're off to church — well, I'm best left to myself when I feel foul.'

'It might help if you came with me to the service at St. Botolph's.'

'No thanks.'

'It'll be quite short — '

'I said no thanks — didn't you hear me?'

'No use for religion, Loraine?'

'Oh my God, what is all this?'

Usually when she was in a black mood he went away. She wished he would go away now but he stayed lolling against the door.

'I like the idea of life after death — '

'I don't. Gives me the shakes. That's what religion does. Gives people the shakes. There'd be a hell of a lot more peace in the world if it weren't for religion. Look at Ireland, India, Israel — anywhere — the whole load of codswallop started when people began to form tribes and had to think of ways of keeping the tribe together with a lot of bloody sanctions. Then of course a god had to be invented and a priesthood to propitiate him to stop him from punishing people who refused to conform to the rules of the tribe. It makes me sicker than the baby did to see folk trotting off to church because they're afraid something foul will happen to them if they don't. Modern people see through it, Harry, and want nothing to do with it, so don't expect me to go to church, ever.

'That was a lovely sermon, Loraine — but perhaps I'd better be off before I wind up in hell!'

'Get knotted!' she shouted after him, but when he'd gone, for some minutes she frowned at the kitchen sink. Yes, it was a lovely sermon. Eric's.

By the time he was back she was in a better temper. She had loosened the zips of her slacks and started preparations for supper.

'I'm making a curry. I'll have a curry if it gives me heartburn all night. I'm sick of the food we have to eat. What couldn't I do to a salmon mousse, or a brandy steak — but a curry will be better than cold spam, for God's sake! You don't look so pleased with yourself as you did when you left. What's up?'

'For one thing I'd like to give you all those things, and more — '

'Oh, for shouting the odds, Harry! You should know by now I don't mean the half of what I say. You've something on your mind. Give.'

'Did you hear the engine when I came back?'

'Yes. Sounded dicey.'

'She's finished. She stopped altogether half way home. I could hardly get it to start again — '

'Does that mean we need a new engine?'

'Something like that. And we haven't the money.'

'Nothing?'

'We owe all we have.'

'My maternity gear must have set us back a bit. What did it cost?'

'Twenty pounds.'

'It's a lot for slacks, a smock and a couple of bras — '

'And we need new tyres too. So I'm going to work.' 'On your book? It's good, Harry, worth trying out — '

'No. We need cash now. So I'm going across the field to see my farmer.'

His card was at the school but he wasn't going to write for it. The farmer was a friendly fellow and would risk using him without it, he hoped.

'Can't I do something?'

'You are. Plenty.'

'Earn something, I mean. Dammit,

other child-bearing women do. I'll be over this phase soon — '

'I'd rather you got me my meals and looked after things and me — '

'Just like a jolly old housewife, eh?'

'Yes,' he answered with a smile. 'If you like to put it that way.'

She might have told him she meant it that way but he had gone off to see his farmer.

There was plenty to do in the chicory fields, with the stock, and around the farm, so the farmer could use him, *sub rosa*, and now every day he was off at half-past six and home dead beat ('looking dead grotty') at half-past five; and in August with various harvests to be got in he often didn't return before ten. He grew lean and she grew stout.

Then in the middle of the month there came a double blow, one foreseen, the other not. He had twice coaxed his engine into Lynn for money or stores; on the third occasion with the cash his solicitors sent him — £10 less than usual — there was a letter to inform him (with regret) that a company had failed and his income was by that amount reduced. And at Docking on the way home the engine packed in altogether. He was near a garage whose owner came with him to the van.

'How many miles have you done in her, maister?'

'She'd done about fifty thousand when I bought her. Well over a hundred and fifty thousand by now.'

The mechanic tried to start her up.

'Reckon you need a new engine, maister.'

'Yes. I've been expecting that. Could you get me a re-conditioned one?'

'I could try, but she's a bit old — the van, I mean — is it worth it?'

'Try, will you.'

'Them tyres won't last much longer. Them two aren't safe in my reckoning. It's a wonder you're allowed on the road — '

'She was tested in January. I have the certificate — but I've travelled a lot since then. You'd better get two tyres as well — '

'I'd make it three if I were you, maister — '

'All right. Three.'

They pushed the van the hundred yards into the garage, and he walked the three miles to camp. She was sitting within the caravan door washing potatoes. He sat down near her his back against the wheel.

'So our poor old van has had it?'

'So have we.'

He handed her the letter. When she'd read it she said,

'Where does the bread come from, Harry? Your income, I mean.'

'Marriage settlement of my grandfather. He was an officer in the old Indian Army. Most of my relatives were in the army. The thing used to produce over a thousand a year. Now it's going to be not much more than seven hundred.'

'And the van?'

'New engine — well, a reconditioned one — and three new tyres. I don't know how we're going to pay.'

Loraine rose and from within the caravan called,

'And when she got there she found the cupboard not quite bare. We've two tins of stew and one of mince, but I'm using the mince for tonight. We've enough sugar and tea to last a week. Nothing else — half a loaf of bread.'

'We'll have to run up bills, that's all.'

'There's something else we could do.'

'What's that?'

'I'm showing now, Harry.'

'Showing? Oh. Yes, I see what you mean.'

She sat down again on the doorstep and watched the struggle going on in him and knew she didn't want him to be hurt by whatever in Kent might be waiting there to hurt him.

'No,' she said. 'It's a corny idea. Scrub it. It won't do the slightest good. I told you — '

'I should have taken you to your mother long ago.'

'Harry, don't let's go! It'll be a waste

of what little money we have. She won't give me a penny — I must have been off my loaf — '

'We're going. Your mother must be given the chance to do what she ought for you. Even if we were rich I would say the same.'

'But Harry — '

'I know what you're thinking. You're thinking that something happened in Kent so I avoid the county. Well, something did happen. I said I'd never tell you what it was but now I know I will. No, not now, but when you've had your baby.'

'Harry, why not tell me now?'

'It's no good, Loraine. I can't tell you until that — that — '

'Bridge is crossed? Water-shed would be the more appropriate term I think!'

'All right. Water-shed. I've made up my mind about it.'

'And nothing will alter it, you obstinate man. It's funny though. I feel the birth of this baby is going to turn into a water-shed for me too, when all sorts of things are going to be resolved.'

'So as soon as we get our van back and some money we'll go.'

'O.K., if you say so, Harry.'

It was awkward not having the van. Loraine was getting over the worst phase of her pregnancy and would like to have varied the simple life with expeditions as they had in May and June to Norwich, Holkam Hall, Burnham Thorpe and Sandringham. However, as August drew to a close she grew calmly content to sit quiet and let her baby grow, advice which the King's Lynn doctor had given her. 'And no liquor' he had said, which was a laugh since they could afford none. It was getting in their supplies which was difficult until the farmer's wife offered to do their shopping for them.

The van was back by the 27th, and he slept in it again. With his August cash he'd paid part of the bill, and from his September money (and his earnings) he paid off the garage and all his debts, leaving him with nine pounds to last until October. On the fourth of the month they struck camp. When all was ready Loraine looked around.

'I wouldn't have thought it possible for me to get sentimental over a field. I must be bonkers!'

But she knew why she loved the little field.

Below Cambridge he was for taking the B1368 but Loraine persuaded him to stick to the A10. If they could get to Kent by noon, she thought, they could quit that county in the afternoon. Near Royston they drew into a lay-by for coffee and sandwiches, sitting in the caravan. Harry got out a map.

'What are you looking for?'

'Leeds.'

'I can direct you — '

'And a possible place for a camp near it.'

'What for? We shan't need one.'

'I might. Your mother hasn't seen you for two years. I've been thinking she might like you to stay around for a while.'

'You think she might ask me to stay?'

'Yes,' he answered. 'That's what she'll do.'

'You're a dream, Harry, you really are! Or living in one — '

Suddenly all around them there was the roar of motor-bicycles. They looked out of the windows to see youths dressed in black leather jackets with crash helmets decorated with a tiger. Harry jumped up, went to his cutlery drawer, took his peeling knife, and opened the caravan door upon which one of the lads was pounding. A lean-faced youth with small black eyes and on his helmet the tiger and the words 'I'm the greatest. Hear me roar', put in his foot.

'Move on, mister.'

'Oh?'

'Don't argue about it. Move!'

'No.'

'Want your caravan smashed?'

The other youths had crowded behind their leader. There were nine of them, all dressed alike, all about eighteen.

'This is our pitch, see? We've a meeting here, see? Every Saturday mornin', see? So move!'

He brought out a knife, flicked it open.

'There's a woman inside expecting a baby. That make any difference?'

'Not a bit it doesn't, mate.'

'I thought it wouldn't.'

'Get them stones, fellers. Smash his windows. Now I'm comin' in, mister, so if you don't want to get hurt — '

'It's you who is going to get hurt,' said Harry.

From behind his back he brought his knife.

'That's done it, mister!' said the leader viciously, and lunged forward, but Harry thrust first and the knife cut the lad's cheek. Blood spurted.

'Yes, it has,' said Harry. 'You take another step and I'll cut you up good and proper. I'll cut you deep. Deep as hell. Now, get out!'

He looked over the leader at the rest, the stones in their hands.

'Out. All of you.'

He didn't shout, but the leader hesitated, muttering as he dabbed his cheek.

'My God, you'll pay for this — '

'No, you will. I'll have you bastards where you belong — back in Borstal, see? Now get out before I lose my temper.'

Loraine had seen something of the iron in him but this . . . his chin was thrust out as firm as a jetty, his eyes narrow, his mouth a slit. And the lads went. Somebody shouted something about him being a ruddy copper, others swore filthily, but their leader was a bloody mess and something had to be done about that so one by one they remounted their bikes and roared off.

Harry shut the door. He washed the knife and sat down. His face was still a frozen mask but he drew the map towards him as though he'd never been interrupted. Loraine stared at him, scared, wondering when the Harry she knew would come back. He said,

'You ought to be able to guess some of my past from that.'

Gradually the strength and hate were peeling away, his eyes softening.

'I'm used to dealing with boys like that. For most of my life I was a teacher in Borstal. Borstal in Kent.'

10

Within her mind the vision of that look on his face Loraine was not surprised he didn't stop in Royston to report the affair to the police. She was ready to believe he was wanted in Kent for murder. When after some time she found her tongue she didn't ask him about Borstal or what he meant nor directly about his action in the affray.

'Those lads frightened me,' she said. She thought of adding that he'd frightened her too, 'But what frightens me now is the fact that nobody stopped. There were hundreds of cars going in both directions but nobody stopped to find out what was going on. Surely somebody must have seen we were in trouble?'

They were waiting at traffic lights when Harry replied,

'Yes, there were plenty of cars but

people always go as fast as possible from point A to point B. Anyway, what was there to see? A man standing at the door of his caravan talking to some lads. Why should anyone stop? Those who noticed us were probably glad to see a caravan off the road. We're not popular with motorists.'

'They ought to have stopped! Somebody ought to have stopped!'

'I might not have stopped myself. Pulling up suddenly on a busy road can be dangerous.'

'Well anyway, I'll stick to your little roads in future,' she muttered.

An hour later they were at the Dartford tunnel in the queue of vehicles going down the ramp: in daylight again and on the A20; off it before long for the byways, and through such places as Kingsdown and Heaversham, and via Borough Green across country to the A274: off that at Langley and so towards Leeds. Half-a-mile from the village he stopped on a wide verge.

'I don't know about this, Harry,' she

said. 'I think it's a mistake. I know my mother. It won't do any good. I told you. I'm sure it won't. I wish we hadn't come — let's go back!'

'Where does your mother live?'

'There are some bungalows. It's a small housing estate the other side of the village. I wish we were a hundred miles away!'

She spoke as though she had no air in her lungs, breath catching, fingers clenching and unclenching.

'You'll feel better with some food inside you. It's time for lunch anyway.'

He detached the caravan while she walked about staring up the lane in the direction of her mother's home. He called her in and made her drink some coffee and eat a sandwich. She said,

'The trouble is kids can't stop fearing their parents. At least I can't. But parents can stop loving their children. When the kids are grown-up parents feel they are free to live their own lives. They don't want the responsibility of kids any more. They've had enough. That's my mother, anyway.'

As he was silent, she said,

'You don't believe that?'

'I don't know yet. Shall we go?'

'What's the time?'

'Half-past one.'

'Then we'd better. She'll be off to her golf soon.'

Before she got into the van she put on her overcoat.

'If I let it hang loose she won't notice,' she said.

Harry would have liked to make a comforting remark but there was nothing he could say: he was realizing what an ordeal this was for Loraine, an unmarried daughter six months pregnant about to meet her mother. He murmured,

'Would you like me to come in with you?'

'I'm not going in alone.'

They drove on until they came to a group of bungalows each one like its neighbour, with short paths up a slope through tiny gardens to their recessed front door.

'See what I mean?' she muttered. 'Respectability in every net curtain.'

'Which is your mother's?'

'That.'

They left the van at the garden gate and walked up the path to the door beneath its fancy brick porch.

'Don't be nervous. I'm here to protect you,' he said as bells chimed when she pressed the button.

'I haven't been here for three years, Harry, and I — I wish — '

The door opened. Mrs Cartright was shorter than her daughter, dressed in brown slacks, brown jumper and peaked grey cap. Her complexion was florid, eyes small and brown, mouth hard.

'Good heavens — so it is you, Loraine! I saw you coming up the path but I couldn't believe my eyes. Now what in the world brings you . . . '

She looked at Harry.

'Now let me see. You are engaged,

aren't you? Well, child, introduce me to your fiancé.'

'Mr Hobart is just a friend, mother — '

'What? Oh. Well, come in. I've a pairs tournament at half-past two so I can't give you long. You've had your lunch I suppose?'

'Yes, thank you,' said Harry.

In the hall there was a brown leather bag of golf clubs leaning against a chair. They went into a sitting-room crowded with furniture brought from other homes.

'That's just as well. I never have more than a snack before a match and couldn't possibly cope with one for you.'

Harry crossed to the fireplace for he had noticed on the mantle a photograph of Loraine taken when she was a young girl. She had hair to her waist. There was another when she was grown up on an occasional table near the window: the hair was short. He could see no portrait of the husband.

'Take your coat off, Loraine, and tell me what you've been up to. I must say this visit is unexpected. I thought you were in London. Did you say Mr Hibbart *isn't* your fiancé?'

'His name is Hobart, Mother. Harry Hobart.'

'Hobart. How do you do, Mr Hobart. But I am a little confused . . . '

She had a rattling, metallic voice. Harry could imagine it going on and on in this room, in other rooms, driving people to do her will.

'Well, I suppose Loraine will tell me where you fit in. Now, Loraine . . . '

She stopped. Loraine had opened her coat.

'Good gracious! You're having a baby — '

'Yes.'

'Very nice too, my dear!'

'I'm not married, Mother.'

'You — what did you say?'

'I'm not married.'

Loraine sat on one of the chairs against a wall. Her mother turned to Harry.

'I hope you can explain what she means.'

'She means what she says, Mrs Cartright. We thought it best you should know — '

'I am sure that was very right and proper since I presume you are the man responsible — '

'No, Mother. Mr Hobart has nothing to do with it. It was Eric — the man I was engaged to.'

'You mean to tell me, Loraine, without getting married you slept with that man and — '

'Yes, Mother. I'm sorry to upset you.'

'Sorry! Sorry, indeed! I'm absolutely disgusted!'

'I've come to you for help.'

'Help?'

'We have very little money, and I thought — '

Loraine swallowed her nervousness.

'Well, we thought perhaps you might take me back here for a bit, or help us with money, or — '

'Mr Hobart,' her mother interrupted.

'You appear to have something to do with this, but I still don't understand where you come in — '

'I met Loraine in a public house in York, Mrs Cartright. I did not know she was pregnant then, but I could see she was distressed so I befriended her.'

'When was this?'

'Last March.'

'March! Where have you been living since then?'

'In my caravan.'

'Both of you?'

'Yes . . . '

'So you and Loraine have been living together for months?'

'Not in the sense you mean,' he murmured.

'A likely tale! You must think me a fool, Mr Hobart.'

She turned on her daughter.

'And now you come to *me* for help!'

There came a tap at the window. Peering in was a woman with a runaway chin and big blue eyes. She was smiling and nodding. Mrs Cartright went to the window, partially opened it and said,

'Go away, Dolly! We're busy — '

'But I thought I saw Loraine — '

'Yes, yes. Later. Perhaps you'll see her later.'

The window was closed.

'I only hope she couldn't see you, Loraine. At least you had the decency to wear your top coat when you arrived.'

She looked at Harry, her eyes like brown pinheads.

'However, it may not matter if she noticed or not. You seem to have made yourself responsible for her, Mr Hobart. I should have thought the decent thing for you to do would be to marry her and make yourself entirely responsible. For the child as well. I suppose I must believe it isn't yours but I can't see that that makes any difference at all under the circumstances.'

'I think Loraine may wish to say something — '

'She has no right to say anything.

She's made a fool of herself with a man, and this is the best way out of it.'

'All right, Mother. I told Harry no good would come of it.'

'Now you listen to me, Loraine. A girl in your predicament has to take the first chance that offers. You marry this man, and be thankful to get out of it so easily. If young people can't control themselves — '

'All right, Mother! You needn't say any more.'

Loraine walked out. Harry said,

'I am sorry we've upset you, but don't worry. I shall be looking after Loraine until her baby comes — '

'I hope you see the sense in what I say, Mr Hobart, and will marry her — '

'I doubt if she'll have me, but still — not to worry.'

He smiled and added,

'Good luck in the tournament!' and followed Loraine to the van where she was talking to the woman who had peered in.

'How are you, Dolly?'

'I still have my migraine, dear, but not so bad as it was. I've found a perfectly marvellous faith healer — is this your husband?'

'Mr Hobart, Miss Fanshawe.'

'How do you do! This *is* exciting! Fancy your mother never telling me you were married, Loraine!' She whispered, 'When is it due?'

'December.'

'I'm so excited for you, Lorry dear!'

Mrs Cartright came out with her golf clubs and went towards her garage. She was looking at and listening to the group on the road.

'Do write to me, dear Loraine! I want to know where you're living now, all sorts of things. I'm so glad you're happy, and having — you know . . . ' Goodbye, Mr Hobart — and Mrs Hobart! Goodbye!'

As they drove off, Harry had a droll expression playing about his mouth.

'You made her happy — '

'Silly little thing. Mrs Hobart . . . I can't think why I didn't disillusion her.'

'You didn't because you didn't want to hurt your mother. She was listening, you know.'

'Rubbish.'

But by the time Harry had hitched on the caravan Loraine was not so sure. She said,

'As I said, kids never really escape from their parents. Perhaps that was why.'

He negotiated carefully the turn into the Maidstone road.

'I think that even the most sophisticated parents never escape from their children either. Your mother was bewildered and hurt in her pride in you — '

'Pride in me? Don't talk such balls, Harry — '

'There were two photos of you in her sitting-room. I bet she boasts about you at her golf club, saying how clever you are and how well you're doing. It was a shock to find things different — I'll bet she's already sorry she was so unsympathetic — '

'Oh to hell with it!' said Loraine. 'For God's sake get me out of here!'

'O.K. I know a place in Essex — '

'Then get me there — fast.'

'Point A to point B?' he said and pressed the accelerator pedal until the needle touched fifty.

'I said *fast*, Harry!'

'There's a legal limit for caravans, Loraine, and this is it,' but he went faster all the same.

She made only one comment as they neared *The Wheat Sheaf* Inn on the outskirts of Maidstone. 'So there you are, Harry: left holding the baby — literally, damn it,' to which he replied,

'It's a good little engine they've put in. I could do seventy without the caravan.'

At the *Wheat Sheaf* they had to bear left through a roundabout before re-taking their road down into the town: as they reached it a Cortina was coming up. A man leaned out. Loraine caught sight of a big, heavy face and a gesticulating hairy arm as the man shouted,

'Hey you! Mr Hobart!'

Harry glanced out. It was Mr Appleton. He accelerated.

'Mr Hobart! Stop!'

Harry drove on, the caravan beginning to sway as he reached fifty-five. In his wing-mirror he could see the car was after him.

'Who is that?'

'Someone I don't want to see.'

'You don't say!'

'Where is he now?'

Loraine half rose and peered out of the back window.

'Catching up.'

Harry swung off the road, up a short slope, and down into the town.

'Now?'

'Still on our trail. There's one car in between us. What's it all about, Harry?'

They reached the traffic lights by the bridge over the Medway. They turned green as they reached them and Harry turned right.

'It said left for London and the A20, Harry — '

'I know but he would have caught us up and we've got to throw him off. Where is he now?'

'Still around. Must you throw him off, Harry?'

'Yes.'

He drove up the High Street to more traffic lights at red.

'How far behind is he?'

'A couple of cars and then a lorry. I think he must be behind that.'

The amber came up and Harry drove on, almost at once turned left.

'Where *are* you going? This is the entrance to the Star Hotel!'

'I know, but there's a way through.'

An attendant in a white coat came running from a hut beyond the covered part of the hotel garage. Harry drove on past him, and down the slope leading out into a street at the back of the hotel. The man was shouting, but, face set, Harry turned left only to be held up once more. As soon as he could he turned into Pudding Lane and so towards the High Street again.

'My God!' said Loraine. 'That — '

But Harry interrupted her saying, 'Can you see him?'

'No.'

'He'll have to come back this way too ... hell, I wish we weren't so conspicuous.'

Hugging the left-hand side of the street, he drove past a cannon, symbol of wars long over, and so back to the lights by the bridge.

'Now?'

'I can't see him.'

It seemed to Harry the lights were going to be for ever red.

'God, I wish they'd change!' he fumed. 'Any sign yet?'

'I think I can see him now. There are some cars and a 'bus in between but I think it's his Cortina.'

The lights changed at last and they drove over the bridge.

'He'll follow you on to the A20, Harry.'

Ahead was a small public house, *The Ship*. Harry turned left, drove through a housing estate, and at the end of it turned right. A few minutes later they were in country lanes. He stopped at a convenient spot a mile further on.

'He'll either have seen which way we went or he won't.'

'I wish you'd tell me what goes on.'

He didn't answer so in silence they waited for ten minutes. Nobody came. Harry sighed.

'We've thrown him off.'

'It looks like it. That going through the hotel was a bit of graft! Well, Harry? What does it all mean? Give.'

'I can't. Not yet. Only trust me, Loraine. Please go on being my friend.'

She put her arm along his shoulder.

'I could be more than that,' she whispered. 'If you weren't such a silly old crap.'

He looked at her, caught by the tone in her voice, saw the expression in her eyes.

'Loraine . . . Loraine . . .'

'Can't you see I love you, you bloody fool? This chase, this — '

'But Lorry, your career — '

'Oh, not any more! Can't you stop being blind for a moment, and love me a little?'

'A little! Oh, my darling — I love you with everything I am. I . . . '

She pulled his head to hers. They kissed, a long, long kiss, and then they looked at one another like bemused children, silent, too joyful for speech, but at last Loraine said,

'God, how I love you, Harry . . . '

'And I you . . . '

They could not get close enough, so sat for many minutes.

'So, Harry? This hairy ape, this silly secret — '

'Not yet, my darling. Don't ask me yet.'

'Must this thing be between us, Harry, even now? It needn't you know.'

'I wish I could be sure of that — '

'Be sure, Harry!'

He shook his head. Loraine sighed.

'O.K., you silly man. Roll on the water-shed — though what difference that's going to make I can't see.'

She stroked the hand she held.

'But at least we don't have to pretend any more, and that's something to be thankful for. And I'm in your care and protection, have been for months — you're lumbered with me for good and with the child I know now I kept because you wanted me to.'

She snuggled against him and he pressed her head into his shoulder . . . and was cruelly reminded of another cropped head that had once been pressed there.

Would she still love him if she knew?

11

As they drove along the quiet lanes of Essex looking for a camping place they were both preoccupied. Loraine was wondering about Harry's past, and Harry, now that he had told her of his love and knew she loved him, whether he ought not to make his confession now. So, silent, they went slowly on. Loraine made up her mind to 'forget it' — Harry would tell her when he was ready: and Harry, because he had planned it that way and was so desperately afraid of losing her, decided again to wait until her baby had been born.

Both ended their private thoughts at the same moment.

'Let's try to find a river — '

'I wish I could work up an appetite — '

Their abrupt bursting into concerted

speech made them laugh. Neither asked what the other had been thinking about. They knew.

Towards five o'clock they came upon a bit of new road, the old corner behind it bordered by a copse. They would camp there for he must go to the nearest village for food before the shops shut.

'We've about five quid to get us to Yorkshire so I can't buy much.'

'The only thing I could eat are a dozen oysters.'

He was back at six — with sausages and a bag of potatoes. She lit a ring, put on the frying pan.

'Sausages. I'm sick of the sight of them. I wish I *could* have a dozen oysters!'

'I know, my darling. But things will improve when we get to Yorkshire — '

'How so?'

'Because there are shops where I can get credit. I might even get you your oysters on tick!'

She stood against the sink her smock

riding up over her belly.

'I think she might have helped. She ought to have helped — '

'Never mind.'

'But I do bloody mind! Not even a tip . . . and you left holding the baby, literally as I said and it's not even yours! God, I wish it were! Harry, sleep in here tonight, will you?'

He wondered about that.

'No, not for that, my lovely one! In any case I feel too foul. If it's not one thing, it's another and now it's constipation . . . I just want you near. Please, Harry.'

'All right.'

He brought in his gear and while she cooked their supper prepared the bunks.

'I could hardly get mine ready last night. Couldn't see to do it. I suppose I still have my feet?'

'Yes. They're still there.'

After supper they strolled hand in hand into the copse. They didn't smoke. They had run out and he hadn't bought any on his shopping expedition.

'I sometimes feel I've been married to you for years, Harry.'

'Me too.'

'I'll get in some flowers tomorrow — '

'That's it! That was one factor, anyway — '

'What are you talking about?'

'I've often asked myself when I fell in love with you. I've thought of all sorts of things but I'd forgotten the flowers. When I left the Langsett site I chucked yours out. But when I was near King's Lynn I got some more. So they must have had something to do with it.'

She squeezed his hand.

'When did you know you loved me, Lorry?'

She thought about it for a long time.

'I don't know. I had to get Eric out of my thoughts first, and that wasn't easy when I'm carrying his kid. With a woman I think it's the physical side of a man that first attracts her — so it may have been when I first saw you stripped.

But all sorts of things have built it up since then. Your — your honesty, integrity. Your determination to do your best for me . . . keeping the baby . . . all sorts of things.'

They reached the lane again and turned back.

'Harry, I must ask you this. Do you mind about the baby? It being *his* baby, I mean, now that you want me as your wife?'

'I asked myself that question one time. It was at Holme, the first time we bathed there. I was talking to myself — I often used to, do still — and I was passing a small boy paddling. I asked myself that question and I said out loud 'I don't care a damn!' The boy looked at me as though I were bonkers. But I don't.'

'Sure?'

'Sure.'

'I always imagined men preferred a virgin — '

'Don't talk such old-fashioned — what's your favourite word?'

'Crap.'

'Such old-fashioned crap! I love you, you as you are, Lorry — what's the joke?'

'You, my sweetheart! Calling *me* old-fashioned. It's an adjective I've often applied to you, isn't it?'

'Not any more?'

'No. Not any more. Modern, unmodern — they don't mean a thing to me now!'

They walked in silence until the caravan came in sight.

'There's our home. There's another question I want to ask, Harry.'

'Yes?'

'When we are married, will the baby be made legitimate?'

'I don't think so, Lorry. I think it'll have to be legally adopted.'

They went to bed early, undressing without thinking about it. He thought her tummy was stretched so it would burst. She scratched it.

'Keep still will you, you little beast! He's kicking like mad tonight, Harry . . .'

He stood beside her in his pyjamas.

'Goodnight, my darling.'

'Goodnight.'

They kissed.

'It's not much of a goodnight kiss that, but I suppose it'll have to do — under the circumstances.'

At dawn there was a mist and it was cold.

'When there's a mist in the morning and the sun sets around half seven I know it's time to make for my winter quarters.'

'The aerodrome near what-is-it?'

'Better than that. We've a long way to go, Lorry. Let's be off.'

Later in the day they were on the B1188 going towards Metheringham. Ahead they saw a girl walking at the side of the road. As they approached, she thumbed a lift. He stopped. The girl came running. She was a coloured girl of twenty-two or three with the rich chocolate skin and large dark eyes of her race.

'Thanks, thanks!' she said. 'It's

getting awful warm for walking. Are you going anywhere near Louth?'

'We can take you a good step on your way.'

'I'm ever so grateful. Shall I ride in the caravan?'

Loraine said,

'I'll come and ride with you and we can talk.'

'It won't be too comfortable. You'll bounce and sway a bit.'

'I'd like it, Harry.'

She'd have a good natter and that would do her good.

'O.K. I'll drive very slowly and if you sit over the wheels you'll not feel it too much.'

They went off and he drove on at between twenty and twenty-five miles an hour. And thought of her, saw her in her black moods and gay, saw her lying beside him on the warm sand, bending over the stove swearing at it because it wasn't capable of cooking what she wanted it to cook, helping him around the caravan and their camps, walking through woods and fields picking flowers — Robert herb, vetch, white bryony, wild foxglove, honey-suckle, willow herb — to make the caravan gay. He saw her from all angles and in all postures, saw her slim in her bikini, big with her child; was with her in the *Bird of Paradise* or in Nelson's church where, for her, she had behaved reverently — but then it was Nelson not God she was in awe of! Saw her being nice to him, saw her being rude; saw her furious when he had suggested she come to St. Botolph's. And knew he loved her because she had brought him back to himself.

He returned to the present to see that his speedometer was touching twenty-five and slowed down. He wondered how they were getting on. They had had half-an-hour together and having had next to nothing for breakfast it was time she had something to eat. He had skirted Lincoln and there was a village ahead. He stopped outside a public house.

They went in. He ordered the drinks and sandwiches and learned that the girl was a nurse. He brought the sandwiches and lemonade to their table and the girl said,

'It's going to be a fine baby I'm sure, Mr Hobart!'

'Sheila says it'll be a girl. She says most first babies are girls and she's handled dozens of them. I've learned a lot about having a baby.'

They ate and drank. Sheila said she was ever so grateful for the lift and insisted on paying for the meal.

'And I've enjoyed talking to you, Mrs Hobart.'

'Not half as much as I have,' said Loraine. With a wink at Harry she added, 'You tell my husband what you told me.'

'Having a baby isn't nearly as difficult as some women think, Mr Hobart. But a woman has got to let herself go, forget she's a lady and all that because when she's giving birth she isn't. She's an animal, a female animal like any other. If she can remember that she'll come through with flying colours.'

'And what about him. What should Mr Hobart be doing? Ought he to be around?'

'I don't like men around when a patient is in labour. They've done their duty nine months before and haven't given it a thought since — or at any time for that matter! I think husbands should go for a walk, or out with the boys, until it's over.'

'How long have you been in England, Sheila?'

'I was born here. I was adopted by a woman, a white woman, who had two children of about my age and had lost her husband.'

'Have you come up against much prejudice?'

The girl thought about it for a moment, said,

'When I was a very little girl in the bath with my white sister I thought I was dirty and tried to scrub myself clean. But my mother — my foster-mother — was a very wise lady and she soon put me right so that I grew up neither ashamed nor proud of the colour of my skin. I think the trouble with many coloured people is self-consciousness. They believe the colour of their skin matters and they can't forget it so they see hostility where there isn't any. Sometimes we get an older woman in who looks at me with a bit of doubt, but I'm friendly and I laugh a lot — and I'm a good nurse too! So . . . ' She shrugged, went on,

'A lot of nonsense is talked about racialism. We're all racialists at heart — it's the tribal instinct and it isn't something you can get rid of easily whatever the politicians say. So . . . but I must be getting on. No, I'll walk. Thanks, thanks, again.'

They waved to her from the door.

'Don't forget to write!' she called.

'I won't. I'll send you our address as soon as I have it.'

'Good luck!'

They returned to the van. He started the engine but didn't let in the gear, said,

'I wonder whether, when you've had your baby, you'll want to go back to your career — you've often talked about it — do you think you will?'

'I don't know now, Harry. All I know for sure is I want you near me.'

She was looking all over his face. He smiled.

'What do you see in me — me, the old 'fuddy-duddy'?'

'I see a *man*, Harry. I see a man neither modern nor old-fashioned, a man of all time — a quiet fellow who belongs to *himself*, and that's something to be thankful for these days, for God's sake!'

Her face was softening as she studied his.

'I also see rather a good-looking guy. Nice, steady eyes, a small, firm mouth. Face a bit too square perhaps — '

'I'm still something of a 'square' still then!'

'And I love him and want to give him a kiss.'

He drew her forward, kissed her passionately, drew back.

'I shouldn't kiss you like that,' he whispered.

'Kiss me again — like that.'

'No — please not, Lorry!'

'My pregnancy, is that it?'

'I'd hate to harm the baby — '

'O.K. Not to worry. I can wait until we're married.'

'I wish I could be sure about that — '

'We'll be married all right. I'm not letting you go now, Harry.'

He hadn't meant that but didn't say so for several men were standing outside the pub, grinning at them. Harry grinned back and let in the gear.

12

They made better time than they thought they would and were in York before six. He had spent some money on petrol, and had exchanged a gas cylinder; now he spent the rest on food.

'I know a good spot near my winter quarters. We'll go there for tonight — '

'Can't we go straight to these 'winter-quarters'? I'm tired, and feeling lousy — '

'I shall have to reconnoitre the place to make sure no one's there. But the place I have in mind for tonight is quite a good one. I'll reconnoitre the other tomorrow.'

'I wish it could be a house. I'm sorry, Harry — I've loved this little home of ours, but — '

'I know. Wait just a little longer and see what I have in store for you, my darling.'

He took the Kirkland road out of York and by half-past seven they were passing through the village of Dendale. Near a cricket field beyond the houses he turned into a gate and descended a slope. There were tall fir and beech trees on one side, the main road parallel to their track on the other. At the bottom of the slope he turned away from the road and drove along a broken concrete lane for a hundred yards.

'Where does this lane lead to?'

'It leads into the grounds of Dendale Manor which is a school. This part of the grounds must be out of bounds for the pupils for I've never seen any of them around. I've heard them yelling at a football match though.'

She uncoupled and he pulled off, turning the van so that they could move off quickly. He then swung the caravan round and stabilized.

He began to wash potatoes: washing rather than peeling made them last longer, but he used his knife for the bad bits of which in this bag there seemed to be a great many.

'I've got some stuff for breakfast but I forgot about tonight. Have we anything to go with these spuds?'

'There's the sausage I couldn't eat this morning.'

She hadn't used the loo properly all day, nor yesterday either, and the jar of petrolager was finished She knew she was turning 'black', and when she was 'black' the world was black.

'I can get credit in Kirkland — that's a nearby market town. I'll get some decent food for you, sweetheart. And living is cheaper in Yorkshire.'

He put the potatoes on to boil and picked up the knife to place it in the drawer.

'I'm sorry I had to cut that kid,' he murmured.

'What kid? Oh, that one. He deserved it.'

'I'm sorry, all the same.'

She was in a mood to be spiteful about that for her tongue was like a bit of felt and she had a headache, and she couldn't eat any supper.

'It'll save time if I look into our winter-quarters tonight.' he said.

'You do that.'

He went away. She sat on her bunk, turned on the radio. The disc-jockey said they were going to enjoy an old-time medley . . . 'tell me you love me even if it isn't true . . . ' She listened for a moment, switched to another channel and for five minutes listened to a talk on exploration, went back to pop before knowing what country was being explored. 'Give me one night of your love till the morning.'

She switched off.

Had she liked these silly songs and the groups that sang them, that still sang them? Yes she had and why the hell not? The only reason why she didn't like them now was because she had become unmodern. That was what going around with Harry had done to her, made her unmodern. And the bloody awful old-fashioned food they ate! Plain, cheap meat, plain puddings, plain ungarnished veg — sausages and mash. One time she had tried to tart the stuff up a bit but for weeks now there hadn't been the cash to buy the extras that could make food palatable.

She went through a menu recollected from the Wyvern: asparagus soup, the real stuff not tinned, Scotch salmon, Norfolk turkey . . . and to finish, deep-freeze raspberries and double cream. In her mind she saw the bright glass, the silver cutlery, the dazzling table-cloth . . .

She thought of her mother in her neat, civilized home and swore at her for not helping her, asked herself if *she* would have taken in a daughter with an illegitimate child on the way and told herself that *of course* she would.

She looked at her watch. He had been gone half-an-hour. He ought to be back. Why wasn't he back?

These 'winter-quarters' of his — another foul camping place miles from amenities where she would prick her bottom every time she went to spend a penny . . . he must sell the caravan. She must persuade him to sell the van and the caravan and hire a cottage, anything, anywhere, so long as she could keep still and be in one place, in a *house*.

She romanticized the cottage they would rent. It was old, but had been renovated. It had a modern kitchen with an electric stove, a 'fridge, and a washing-up machine. And a clothes washer, too. There was a living-room with oak beams across the ceiling and a wide open fireplace and big logs merrily burning. Upstairs there was a bath-room, and nice bedrooms with lattice windows and in one of the rooms a double bed: a beautiful soft modern bed and in that beautiful bed she would have her baby.

She thought of Eric and was in a blind rage with him. For three minutes she used every swear word she could think of about him, and felt better through the stimulation of rage. How could she ever have loved that bastard?

Harry was fifty times the man Eric had been — fifty million she had rated him. Harry would go to Heaven. Eric could go to hell. She hoped there was such a place.

Where was Harry? Why the devil didn't he come back? He'd been gone three-quarters of an hour.

She would have liked a drink, a double gin and tonic, and two or three more after that. She wondered if there was any sherry left. In their early days in Norfolk they'd had an occasional bottle of Empire. She considered looking for it in a cupboard but remembered she'd finished it in a sauce months ago.

She lit a cigarette which made her feel guilty because it was the fourth of the day but told herself she'd blow a tube if she didn't have a fag: and thought about nappies. Before Christmas she would be washing nappies and there would be three of them in this bloody caravan. And the baby would look like Eric: first babies, according to Sheila nearly always resembled their father. So it would have blonde hair with bulbous periwinkle blue eyes and she would have Eric around for ever.

How absolutely bloody.

When a quarter of an hour later he returned she was crying.

'Sorry to have been so long — '

'Where the devil have you been?' she wailed. He knelt beside her taking her hands.

'I had to make sure everything was O.K. I'm sorry, darling. I shouldn't have been so long.'

'I hate it, hate it! I can't go on like this!'

He stroked her cheeks and her hair.

'Look, Lorry — I've brought you something.'

'All I need is gin — and a dozen oysters.'

She was cheering up through his presence and his gentle touch.

'We'll have oysters tomorrow. We'll pop into York — '

'We'll do nothing of the sort! Absolutely crapulous idea when you know very well we can't afford it.'

She blew her nose.

'I'm sorry, Harry dear. I've been brooding and that's a very silly thing to do. It's this foul constipation. What have you brought me?'

He brought out six Victoria plums from his pocket.

'The wasps had got most of them, but they're jolly good. Try one.'

She did.

'Yummy, yes! They are good. Give me another. Where did you get them?'

'You'll see tomorrow. There are still some left.'

She ate two more and while doing so said,

'I've been in a black mood, Harry. It may be partly constipation but I can't have the baby here, Harry, you must see that.'

'You're not going to have the baby here. Look, sweetheart, I've looked after you pretty well so far, so don't worry

190

— not to worry about December. I have my plans.'

She gazed at him wondering what he meant.

'What's this famous winter-quarters like? Will I have to sit on a thistle when — '

'You won't! You'll see. Everything is fine there, and we'll go their first light. For now I think we'd better go to bed. Another plum?'

'I'll eat it for breakfast. I shall be glad to be in the dark,' she said. 'I'm not a sight to be seen by any man, or woman either for that matter. I'm nothing but a damn gipsy. Get me down my hair-brush will you? I can at least brush my beautiful long hair!'

It came over the collar of her smock and she brushed it so that it curled up, and went on brushing it when he turned out the light. By the glow from the paraffin stove they undressed.

'Have you any money at all, Harry?'

'No. I spent the rest on bread, milk, butter, a cereal, etcetera. But I'll get some more in York.'

'When?'

'On the second of October.'

'And this is the fifth of September — how are we going to live until then?'

'On tick.'

'I suppose,' she said, very small. 'You wouldn't sell this caravan and rent a cottage?'

'Well, not yet. Not unless I have to.'

After some minutes in their bunks she said,

'Give me another kiss, Harry. I've been so miserable. You won't ever leave me, will you?'

'Never in this world,' he said as he turned out the stove.

As next morning there was again a mist they didn't set off until eight and stopped in Kirkland at a grocer's.

'The more you buy,' he said, returning with a full bag. 'The more they'll give you credit.'

They left the market-town heading north; after a mile or two he turned into a lane.

'This is a terrible road for the next half-mile. All potholes. I'll go very slowly.'

It was hardly a road at all, just a track which at some time had been ballasted here and there with rough stone from the quarry they skirted. In parts it descended steeply, the van lurching along, the caravan too.

'It's tricky this, but improves soon. I guess this part of the road catches the full force of the winter storms.'

'I hope it leads somewhere — '

'Of course it does! It leads to my house — '

'House!'

'Isn't the view magnificent?'

They were on the side of a deep dale, the tree-covered hill across the valley sparkling in the morning sun. There were no houses to be seen anywhere.

'Beautiful — you didn't say a house, Harry?'

'I said a house, but don't think of it too grandly although it is a grand house. I call it Dotheboys Hall. As far as I can tell no one has lived in it for ages. It's lost away at the head of this dale, miles from anywhere, no other place to be seen — '

'Not furnished I suppose?'

'No. I take everything out of the caravan, bunks, table, carpets, lights — the lot. And there's a junk shop in Kirkland where I hire a few things — hold tight!'

They lurched in and out of a pothole.

'I found it when I first camped where we were last night. I took this lane only to see where it led to.'

They came to a gate with a faded notice — PRIVATE. Keep out.

'Useful that notice! I was as nervous as a rabbit when I first drove beyond it but went on and on until I came upon this mansion. I was so surprised, I had to examine it. I went all around and found a loose catch to a cellar window, used my knife and got in. Some of the rooms are in a pretty bad state but not where we shall be. We occupy the south wing — '

'As non-paying guests!'

'Yes. We shall be near the kitchen — '

'Is there a usable stove?'

'It's an old-type range, but I use it.'

'And no one ever comes?'

'No one. As a matter of fact I know of a number of houses, big places no one wants where it would be possible to stay. There's one in Cheshire. I thought of going there after leaving Sheffield but the last time I went to it I found it full of tramps. One of them told me there were these empty houses all over England; others mentioned ones in London but not many tramps go to them because of the squatters. I asked them to tell me the location of the country ones but they wouldn't. I don't blame them. I didn't tell them about Dotheboys Hall!'

They were passing through a wood of oak, elm, birch, and occasional rowan, all in their bright autumn livery. Pigeons flew and a minute later they came to the house. It stood at the end of a short drive with outbuildings opposite it. It was a big house, a very big house, a mansion as he had said, of grey stone and tall stone chimneys.

'Who would build a house right at the end of a lost valley like this?'

'Some eccentric I imagine, but there it is, solid as a rock.'

He left the van.

'I'll go and open the door.'

Loraine got out slowly. There was something so comical about driving up to this enormous house with the intention of occupying it that even her body felt light.

'Here I am — down those steps.'

She walked carefully over moss-covered flags to the door he held open. He was grinning like a schoolboy.

'I'll fetch a stool,' he said.

She went in, found the big kitchen with the old-fashioned range. He came back with the stool.

'This way.'

He led her down a passage and into a large room. It had bay windows overlooking the valley, and smaller windows on either side.

'The sun shines in here in the afternoon, making it warm — '

'It's not at all damp or cold now.'

'No. This wing is built mostly of timber. The rest of the house is of stone. Do you like the room, Loraine? There are fifteen others to choose from!'

'It's a lovely room. Is there a lavatory?'

'What an extraordinary question!' he said.

Ten paces from her room, in a recess, there was a 'loo' which, he said, was as good as any in Buckingham Palace: indeed, it was better, for over it it had an armchair-looking object with a basket-work lid.

'What an extraordinary loo! And you mean to say it works?'

'It will when I turn the water on — '

'Then I'm going to use it right now. Those plums — much better than oysters!'

He went off to see that the cistern

flooded and when she came out she said,

'Thank God for that! I feel a new woman. Now I suppose you'll tell me there's a bathroom that works too?'

'Five actually, but I only use the one up these back stairs. I'm afraid you can't have a bath every day. We don't want the local water-board investigating. For most purposes I fetch water from the well.'

Loraine was playing with an electric light switch in the kitchen.

'They had an engine one time. Lots of old houses did at the beginning of the century — but wait a while. I've a lot to do before we're properly installed.'

He found paper which he screwed up small, and, from a store he had somewhere in the house, a little kindling. Then he brought from the cellar a bucket of smokeless fuel, furnacite.

'I hate this moment of lighting the stove. Too much smoke for too long and someone might see it. That's why I use furnacite. Fortunately I got in a lot last year — I must have transported over a ton in hundredweight sacks . . .'

He laid and lit the fire-box in the old range, put on the solid fuel. She watched the fire. He ran out: came back.

'Smoke not too bad. I reckon she'll smoke for about ten minutes, then she'll go like a bomb — heats the water, too. Not very well, but still.'

'Has anyone ever noticed the smoke?'

'Not so far — she's picking up now.'

The furnacite began to glow. Loraine sat on the stool and stretched out legs and arms towards the fire. Bone empty, bare as a barn, miles from anywhere — she was in a house!

She hardly saw Harry for the next three hours. He was going backwards and forwards from the house to the caravan. He stripped it of its bunks, its table, its ceiling light, its curtains — everything except the lavatory and the stove. When he'd done that he set up one of the bunks in Loraine's room with the strip of carpet beside it. He asked her if she was happy to have a room of her own for a while. She said yes as long as he wasn't far away, so he fixed the other bunk in a room across from the kitchen. Next he brought a wooden block which he screwed into a beam in the kitchen ceiling, and on to that he fastened the ceiling light from the caravan.

'Not electric light?'

He winked, and wired up the fluorescent tube to a length of cable he'd brought in and linked that to his spare battery, with a switch screwed into the wall beside it.

'Now try,' he said.

The tube flickered and came on. Loraine laughed until she thought she would lose the baby.

'Winter quarters — oh Harry, Harry, you fabulous man!' she said and kissed him.

'The light will last quite a long time

then I swap batteries and get one re-charged.'

He went off on further chores and she returned to her room and looked out of the windows with their view across the dale. It was beautiful. Close to the house but below — for the mansion had been built on the hillside — there was what once had been a fine garden now overgrown with elder and bramble, the lawns a mass of molehills. Around the main windows of her room there was a seat still white from painting of long ago and Loraine sat there and looked about the room he had chosen for her. The floor boards were bare except where he'd put her bunk and carpet but the room had a good shape, longer than it was across. One of the smaller windows overlooked a bastion of another part of the house: the opposite one looked over a walled kitchen garden. This too was overgrown but she could see where he'd got the plums for there were, as he had said, a few left at the top of the tree.

For six months she'd been in the cramped space of a caravan, now she could go from one room to another, could go up and down stairs ... *she was in a house.*

She set out to explore, walking through a stone-flag hall and into a room which was narrow with white and gold panels. From it she could see the side of her own room. She found a wide stone staircase and went up very slowly her hand on the banister savouring the experience. On the first floor there were six big rooms, some facing north towards the hillside, the others south across the valley. There were many passages and many other rooms: in one or two there were pools of wallpaper and plaster, and in one the whole corner of the ceiling had fallen. She didn't go to the second floor; she had already lost her way in the labyrinth of corridors, but came upon a flight of wooden stairs, and heard him below. She descended and found him carrying in the last of the saucepans and cutlery.

'I can't believe it! It's not real! I'm not real! Wake me up, Harry!'

'I'm glad you like it.'

She put her arms about him.

'You're a fabulous feller, Harry! I'd like to hug you but I can't get close enough. We'll try sideways, shall we?'

Each time he went away for their essential living, he brought back things for her comfort — chairs, candlesticks, vases, table-cloths . . . She scolded him for it, saying she didn't need them. One day he brought back a round-back Victorian chair. Its padding was showing through the ancient satin but it was comfortable.

'I don't need it, Harry darling! And we can't afford it — how have you paid for all these things anyway?'

'I haven't. They're from that junk shop in Kirkland. The old man who runs it lets me take a few things, then I give them back when I go, and he makes a charge of a pound or two. So I don't have to pay until we leave. It's only stuff he can't sell easily.'

'This chair, though. You've bought it, haven't you?'

'Yes.'

'It's a good antique, Harry — we had something like it at the Wyvern.'

'Yes, well . . . but I won't have to pay for it before December — '

'How much?'

He stretched his mouth and murmured,

'Ten pounds.'

'Harry! We can't afford ten pounds! We've a baby to consider!'

She shook her head at him. Like a husband caught out in an extravagance he made an excuse to make himself scarce and said,

'I planted some potatoes last March. I'll go and dig some of them up.'

13

As the days shortened and it grew cold with wind and rain he brought the paraffin stove into her room so that when she awoke the room was warm. She dressed while he cooked the breakfast. She cooked the other meals. On fine days he worked in the walled garden finding vegetables to eat (stinging nettles should be on the menu at the Savoy, she averred) and at other times was away in Kirkland getting supplies. She didn't go with him but when the sun shone walked about the estate, or sat in the garden. He had found an ancient iron chair with a round seat and placed it with its back in an angle of the house, and on sunny afternoons she sat there imagining herself a Victorian lady.

'Good afternoon, Taylor,' she would address the gardener whom she vividly saw with whiskers and corduroy trousers tied at the knee.

'Afternoon, marm.'

'How is Mrs Taylor and the children?'

'As well as can be expected, marm, with fourteen mouths to feed and only fifteen shillin' a week.'

'You mustn't talk like that, Taylor, or I shall tell my husband you're a socialist.'

They had a giggle when she recounted her conversations to Harry over their supper.

Often she merely sat, inside or out according to the weather, placid as a cow letting her baby grow. Then, dreaming, she would see again the deep countryside of England, the miles of lonely lanes, the camps they had made, and be glad to be *still*, glad to be waiting for December with Harry to look after her. Apart from some backache she suffered no discomfort now and enjoyed the food she prepared for them on the range.

From his junk shop he brought her a bundle of books, old-fashioned novels which she read at first with amusement only to pass the time; but then re-read them learning from them of a gentler life, of men and women so different from any she had known, and began to doubt that this modern life was so good after all: this brittle life of sophistication and smartness, so smart in dress and tongue and morals, so clever, clever and bitchy. The permissive society — but it wasn't that, it was a *juvenile* society, with adults filled with a worship of the immature, and a frenetic desire to be bang on, swingingly with it, like children grinning in their jungle of the rude. But there was a half-way house between the life she had known and loved and the life she had been reading about, and Harry lived in that house. He would be recognized as a good man a thousand years hence, or a thousand years ago.

She wrote to Sheila and her mother. Harry looked surprised.

'It's all right, Harry. I can be nice too now. In fact, I don't think I could be nasty to anybody any more. I've given the Kirkland Post Office as our address but I don't expect to hear from her. Nor Sheila really.'

They were sitting in the kitchen close to the glowing range, the electric light on, ignoring the bitter rain beating against the windows. The letter-writing finished.

'Mind if I switch off the light, Lorry? This battery is getting low and the other is being re-charged. They told me I'll have to have a new one so this battery must go back into the van tomorrow.'

He switched off the light. The fire seemed to jump to greet them.

'I try not to worry about money, Harry. I'm used to being poor now but food isn't cheap, particularly the nice things you've been getting me. One way and another you must have spent an awful lot. And now you have to have a new battery — will that cost a lot?'

'I'm not sure. VAT might make a difference — I expect I could get one for about nine pounds — '

'Have we got it?'

'Well no — I've about seven, I think.'

'What about our December money?'

'We owe the lot — but we must live — '

'We must also prepare for the baby, Harry.'

'Yes. I saw a doctor in Kirkland this morning. He said to bring you in — '

'But I'm all right, Harry, and it's not due for a month — '

'He said to bring you in. When I told him you'd not been seen by a doctor since July he nearly — what's the expression you use? — nearly blew his tube. Anyway, I've made an appointment for tomorrow afternoon.'

'But — '

'But me no buts, my darling. Actually, he wanted to send the district nurse but I had to persuade him that wasn't necessary but he wasn't pleased. And there are things only a doctor can arrange, Lorry.'

'All right, Harry, whatever you say.'

He put on a kettle, made a pot of tea. It was eight o'clock, pitch dark, with the wind rising.

'I suppose the doctor will get me into a maternity place somewhere. At one time I wouldn't have cared two pins but now I'm yours, Harry, I hate the idea of being a Miss among the Mrs — '

'I don't see why you should be. I said you were my wife.'

'Can we get away with that, do you think?'

'I don't know.'

He washed their cups and the teapot at the sink.

'Don't let's disillusion him about that tomorrow, Harry, even if one day we'll have to. Let's wait until nearer the time. I want to enjoy the fancy that I can go into hospital as your wife as long as possible!'

'O.K. We'll play it off the cuff — right?'

'Right.'

He kissed her, roughing the hair at the back of her neck.

'It'll be down to your waist by the time you're my wife,' he said, adding, 'It's bedtime. I'll light your candle.'

She went to her room where she lit the other candles while he sat on before the fire, staring at the chink of glowing cobs. He felt sad. This baby, her baby — so much depended on him to see that she had a safe confinement. He had sometimes dreaded lest something go wrong, that she have a miscarriage, and at those times his 'winter-quarters' had seemed a dangerous and a stupid place to bring her. But it was not only that which was depressing him. It was what was going to happen after the birth. Would that birth be a kind of death for him?

He heard her coming back. She knelt beside him and took his hand.

'I've been wishing I hadn't agreed to you sleeping in another room. I've been missing our little talks when in bed at night. Do you miss them, too?'

'Yes. Would you like me to move my bunk in?'

'Yes — don't trouble tonight, Harry darling. Tomorrow, though. I've only come back to get another kiss! I love you so much, Harry.'

The one half of her face was red in the firelight. He kissed first her warm cheek, then the cooler, then her lips.

'And I love you too, my darling . . . my sparrow.'

'Sparrow?'

'I used to think of you as a sparrow that had flown in at my window to lighten my darkness. Will you always love me, Lorry?'

'Always, always — never doubt it. So I'm a London sparrow, am I?'

'No,' he said, stroking her hair. 'A golden one!'

14

When the doctor examined Loraine for the second time, he said,

'I'm not too happy about the position of the baby. When your husband came to see me first I got the impression that you were caravanning in a not very accessible spot. I'd rather have you handy, Mrs Hobart. Let me see. The baby is due as far as we can tell on the tenth. I'd like you in the county hospital early next week. What about Monday, December the seventh?'

They looked at one another.

'When I first came to see you I talked of Loraine as my wife. It's hard to explain — it just came out — I did it without thinking — '

'What are you talking about? What do you mean?'

'I mean she isn't my wife.'

The doctor, who reminded them of

the young Mr Bannister, frowned.

'You'd better explain yourselves.'

Loraine said,

'I am not Mrs Hobart. I'm sorry I said I was, but now that it's — well, that arrangements have to be made we know you must be told the truth. My name is Cartright. I am Miss Cartright. Mr Hobart has been looking after me.'

'Then why not get married? If you get married now it would make the baby legitimate and save a lot of trouble — or are you so modern you don't believe in marriage?' he added.

'It's not that. You see . . . Mr Hobart isn't the father.'

They wondered what he would say to that. It being the first time they had faced the realities of their situation they didn't know what to think of it themselves.

'You are a pair of idiots, aren't you?' he said. 'So, Miss Cartright, this man took you under his wing when you were pregnant? Very good of him, no doubt, but what about the man responsible? Any use getting in touch with him? No? Well, all I can say is you seem to get on well together. You've acted with me as man and wife, so why not make it legal? If you were married — there's a registry office here in Kirkland — it would save no end of complications. And money. As your wife, she could get a maternity grant on your National Insurance card —'

'I haven't one.'

'What?'

He was annoyed again. He turned to Loraine.

'Have you an Insurance Card?'

'Yes. It's in my overcoat pocket, Harry.'

'Let me see it.'

Harry fetched her coat from the waiting-room, and handed him the card.

'I see this is stamped only to the end of April, and there are a couple of weeks missing before that. That's nearly eight months without a stamp . . .

didn't you ever try to get unemployment benefit. You might have been entitled to it — '

'I never thought about it.'

'Well, you might not have been lucky. I'm not sure about these things, but as far as I know you have to show willingness and availability to work, which I presume you were not. So that's no good.'

He handed the card back and sat back in his chair, and putting his fingers together, said,

'I doubt if you could get a grant on it, either. It's possible I might be able to wangle sickness benefit — but I wish you'd do the sensible thing and get married. Mr Hobart, you must have had a card at one time! If you've lost it you know you can always apply for another — '

'There are difficulties — '

'All right, all right!' said the doctor, very angry. It was a moment or two before he controlled himself. 'Now listen. Your private affairs are nothing to do with me. Mrs or Miss or whatever you prefer to call yourself, I can give you a Certificate of Confirmation, and you can get a form from the Social Security people and fill it in in one name or the other. That's up to you. But what arrangements am I to make? I want to do the best for you and the baby. There's a place for unmarried mothers near York — '

'No, please not that — '

'Good God, woman! You're going to have a baby! Do please have some sense! Your confinement may not be easy . . . or do you want a private nursing home? Is that it?'

They wondered about that.

'Look,' he said, trying to be less annoyed with them. 'I think it would be best if I forgot what you've said and carried on treating you as a private patient. My secretary has the name Mrs Hobart in her file. All right. As far as I am concerned that is your name and my job is to see that you have an easy confinement in a proper place. There's a very decent little nursing-home in Scarborough. I could get you in there. It's called the Wyvern — what are you grinning at?'

'It's the name!'

'What's wrong with the name?'

'It's a coincidence, that's all. The baby was conceived in a hotel called the Wyvern.'

The doctor didn't smile. He had thought them foolish and pathetic: now he was finding them childish as well.

'You could call that a coincidence, if it mattered,' he said. 'But what do you want me to do? Shall I 'phone the Wyvern?'

'How much will it cost?'

'If you are there a week and if there are no complications I don't see why the bill should come to more than about forty-five to fifty pounds.'

Harry was working out in his head what he could expect from the sale of the vehicles.

'I don't think — ' Loraine began but he interrupted her.

'Make the arrangements please, Dr Wilson. You would like her to go in on Monday?'

'Yes. Mind you, I can't be sure she'll be there only a week — '

'That's all right. I'll take her to the Wyvern on Monday.'

'I shall book her in under the name Hobart — and I only hope I shan't get into trouble over it.'

'That's the name you have on your books, Doctor!'

'Well yes, that is so,' he said with a small smile. 'Here's the address.'

They didn't go to the Social Security office. They didn't think about it. As Harry took the lane at a snail's pace Loraine said,

'Conceived in the Wyvern and born in a place of the same name . . . well, I think it funny, anyway! But Harry, we can't possibly afford a nursing home!'

'I should be able to get at least fifty pounds for the caravan, and if we need any more I'll write to the solicitors . . . '

But he was not sure that legally they

could make an advance. Loraine said,

'But Harry — it's our home! You can't sell our home!'

'It's your life, and the baby's — but I thought you wanted me to sell it?'

'No. Not really. Not our home, Harry.'

The sky had clouded over, a leaden sky with a northeast wind.

'If he knew where we really live!'

'He'd have me shot. However, on Monday you'll be safe and sound in a real house and in a comfortable bed and having lots of good food.'

'I shan't like that not knowing if you're looking after yourself properly.'

But by the Saturday he had some doubts about getting her into Scarborough. It had snowed every day, and every day he went out with his shovel trying to keep a passage clear to the main road but on Saturday he found deep drifts across the exposed section of the track.

'Is it bad, Harry?'

'Not too bad,' he said cheerfully.

'And look, the sun's coming out!'

The storm clouds were drifting away and the red morning sun was struggling through the last of them. But Loraine felt it was the baby and not she who was jumping with anxiety.

On the Sunday morning he was up at six. He went outside. The stars shone fiercely in a clear sky and it was freezing. He went in, stoked the fire, lit and carried the paraffin stove into their room, made himself margarine sandwiches and a cup of tea. At half-past six he was outside again with his shovel.

At nine o'clock Loraine was watching him from one of the upstairs windows. She had brought up a chair and sat close to the window a part of which she had cleaned with her handkerchief. She could see him far up the lane digging and shovelling like one possessed. The sun was shining on the snow and on his bare back. His shirt, his techni-coloured shirt, was draped over the stone gate-post to the drive.

Dear Harry . . . what is it that made

him still withdrawn from her although they knew they loved one another? Silly man! As if whatever it was mattered. It wasn't important, and when he might start to tell her, as he had said he must at the 'water-shed', she would put her finger on his lips and tell him she didn't want to know.

At ten o'clock she saw him thrust his shovel into the snow and begin to walk back for his snack: at the same moment she had a sudden, excruciating pain. It was so severe she gasped, doubled up with it. She bit on her sleeve, fought the pain, sweat on her forehead and hands, until at last it lessened, the terrible knots in her womb untied. She rose very slowly and slowly descended the main staircase and round into the kitchen as he came in at the back door.

'Harry . . . '

'What is it? You look ghastly — '

'I'm afraid it may have started.'

He involuntarily glanced out, thinking of the long length of lane he hadn't cleared. He said,

'Pack your things. I'll start the van.'

They set off at a quarter past ten and managed to get half way up the lane before they stuck. He jumped out and shovelled the snow away from back wheels and front while Loraine sat very still dreading a recurrence of the pain: to have the baby now, here . . .

'It's no good. I'll have to get help.'

'Don't leave me!'

'My darling, I must. Remember what Sheila said? Didn't she say you won't be having the baby at once just because you've had the first pains? It may be days yet — well, hours anyway. I'll be as quick as I can.'

He left her with dread in his heart, running and stumbling in the snow, falling through it into the holes, getting up again, running on until, sweat dripping, he reached a farm on the main road. He banged on the door, and when it opened could hardly speak.

'It's — it's my wife. She's expecting a baby. We're stuck in the snow. The doctor — Doctor Wilson — she's had her first pains. I must get her to him at once.'

It was a big man in his shirt sleeves who had opened to his knock.

'Stook, are thee? Wharm's thee stook, likely?'

'Not far — that lane — '

'Lane below t'quarry?'

'Yes.'

'What thee doin' there?'

'Camping. Please hurry. You have a tractor — ?'

'Campin'? At this time o' year? Fooney time to be campin' any road. Fooney place too.'

He smoked his pipe.

'Please hurry. My wife's all alone, and — '

'It'll cost thee soomthin', on a Soonday and all.'

'Yes. Yes, that's all right — '

'Timmy!'

A tall lad with a ruddy complexion and blue eyes came to the door.

'What is it, Dad?'

'Feller says he's stook. Quarry lane.

Git t'tractor. His woman's havin' a babe, seemingly.'

Loraine saw them coming. It had been only half-an-hour but had seemed the longest wait in her life.

Before they had the rope fixed to the front axle of the van, in turning the tractor nearly slid off the lane, but Timothy — who was full of jokes — righted the movement and little by little pulled the van out of the deep snow into which it had settled, pulled it slowly up the lane, the tractor's huge wheels often racing. When they stuck Harry shovelled away the snow, and the deep treads regained a grip and they went on, the van lurching and swaying but Loraine experienced no further pain. They reached the road at last.

'You'd best git her in to Dr Wilson, reckon,' said Timmy. 'Y' c'n pay leighter.'

'I'll do that. Thanks a lot — '

'Mi moother'll want to knoo how it goes. S'long!'

225

The main road had been cleared of the worst snow, and they were at the doctor's surgery within ten minutes. Harry knocked on the door, and then on the door of the doctor's house nearby. There was no reply. Behind the house was the church.

'I expect he'll be there.'

The pews were half empty, so he saw the doctor and his family at once. He walked up to him as the small congregation rose to sing a psalm, tapped him on the shoulder, whispered . . . '

'When?'

'An hour, about.'

The doctor came out with him.

'I'll have a look at you but I expect you'll be all right,' he said to Loraine. 'Come into the surgery. You both could do with a wash and brush up. What have you been up to?'

'Got stuck in the snow. A farmer pulled us out.'

He unlocked the surgery and showed them where to go for a wash. Ten minutes later he came to Harry and said,

'It may not be long — it's lucky I rang the nursing-home soon after you left. They're expecting her tomorrow, but I expect today will be all right. As a matter of fact if it hadn't snowed I was coming out to see exactly where you were living.'

He didn't add anything to this, but took them into his house where in a sitting-room, which Loraine thought was like the living-room of her imagined cottage, he gave them coffee and biscuits.

'Babies always come either on a Sunday or in the middle of the night — some thoroughly inconvenient time.'

He smiled.

'We start making trouble for one another even before we're born.'

'Will it be all right if I go back to see the farmer — ?'

'You do that, Mr Hobart. It's no good a man hanging about. I'll take your — er — wife in.'

'That's very good of you — is that all right with you, Loraine?'

'Yes, Harry. Of course. Nothing can go wrong now.'

'I'll come into Scarborough this afternoon, Doctor — '

'We may not have anything to tell you, but do that, if you like.'

The doctor's mini was beside the kerb of the little green where he lived. Harry took Loraine's suitcase and put it in the boot. He helped her in, stood irresolute as the doctor got in, moved his hand as she went away, Loraine waving back. When they had quite gone he walked unsteadily to his van, crawled into the back and there lay trembling with exhaustion and reaction. Shivering as though he had a fever, after ten minutes he put himself behind the wheel and as the people in the church were coming out drove away.

He returned to the farmyard and was glad when the farmer and his son came out to him for his legs felt weak.

'I'm very grateful for what you did

this morning — '

'Missus all reight?'

'Dr Wilson has taken her to hospital.'

'I'll tak' three pun, then.'

'I have my jacket down at the house — '

He bit off the word but the farmer heard it.

'House? House did 'ee say? I thought it wore fooney thee sayin' thee was campin' and only a van to show fur it. So thee's bin campin' in t' big house at end of t' lane, is it?'

'Yes. Does it matter? It's empty.'

'How did thee git in, like?'

'Found a window open — '

'T'owner won't be pleased — '

'The do say as owner has — '

'Hold thi noise thoo gawmless donnat!'

Timmy shut his mouth.

'Ah'm thinkin' ah'll heve t' report it like . . . howsome-ever, I c'n see thee's all in what with the snow and the wife bearin' — what about mi mooney? Would thee heve enough?'

'I don't know — '

The farmer looked him over.

'Aye, skint as a mouse I'll be bound. But I'll say no more about breakin' and enterin' if tha bring me five pun tomorrow — '

'Five? But you said — '

'Five pun, mister. Tomorrow.'

A woman came to the door.

'Your dinner's ready,' she called.

It was easier getting back for the snow was hard-packed by their passage over it that morning, and it was downhill all the way. The first thing he did was to look into his wallet to see what money he had. He wouldn't have five pounds but hoped to find one note, but there were no notes. Apart from a few coins in his trouser pocket he had no money at all.

15

There were some potatoes and carrots in his storeroom and a portion of corned beef in the larder. He started to peel the potatoes but felt so ill he gave up. He had some aspirin and he swallowed three with water, and lay on Loraine's bed, covering himself with her blankets and his overcoat. His head ached.

'I shan't get out of here without paying that man. He'll have to buy the caravan.'

He wondered what the farmer would give for it, hoped for the fifty he'd thought. He'd ask the garage in Kirkland to make an offer for the van — another fifty? But if he sold the caravan it would mean rooms . . . would the nursing-home prosecute if he couldn't pay? Prosecute . . . prosecute . . .

He slept like a dead man and when he awoke it was pitch black night. He lit the candle on the floor beside the bunk and found the time was half-past two. He'd promised Loraine to return in the afternoon; she would be wondering what had happened to him — but it was no good worrying about that. The baby would have been born and she would have that to comfort her. He'd best pack up, get to her as soon as possible.

He was the better for his long sleep. He put on a kettle, and shaved: made some tea and corned beef sandwiches, and set to work, munching the sandwiches as he moved around. First he dismantled the two bunks, put them ready by the back door. He also stacked there all the furniture he'd acquired, then, his coat over his head for the wind had backed to the west and it was raining, used her torch to get to the shed where he'd parked the caravan, pulled it out, and placed it above the steps down to the back door. As he worked he thought constantly of Loraine: was she all right? Would she at that moment be nursing her baby? Did women feed their babies directly they were born? He imagined her doing so . . . Few young women seemed to think of their breasts as life-giving for their infants — or perhaps they did and it was men who made them forget it so that some women did fantastic and stupid things to make their breasts attractive, not for their babies but for men.

He lit the gas in the caravan and carried first his bunk then Loraine's into it. It took him the next hour to screw them both back into place. After this he dismantled and reinstalled the fluorescent tube: this was a long job too. It was five o'clock when he finished but still black as pitch outside. He looked around; everything was ship-shape again in his little home. He said,

'And now old friend you'll have to go.'

He was caught by a sudden sadness,

his heart torn by a thin, sharp claw of foreboding. He sat on her bunk, sick with fright, sure that Loraine was dead. His golden sparrow was dead and he was back again in the darkness, in as black a night as that outside. He seemed to know that beyond doubt this was the end: so sat for hours, it seemed, unable to throw away his aching misery: at last slowly climbed from it as from a pit.

'It isn't Loraine. She'll be all right. It's having to sell the caravan . . . '

Gradually the blackest of his despair faded as now the night was fading with above the eastern hills thin streaks of light. He roused himself and got on with the work. He extinguished the gaslight, left the caravan to find that the rain had stopped. He re-entered the house and lit the rest of his candles whose gentle light cheered him. He carried their bedding into the van, then the furniture, last of all the Victorian chair. The furniture, such as it was, had helped to make the place a home, but the chair had done more than that: seeing her sitting in it was like seeing his wife. It too would have to go; but Loraine had talked of one day re-covering it with satin . . .

Everything done, he took a candle and went round the rooms. By the light of his candle they looked more than ever forlorn. For a little while he and Loraine had brought some of them to life — perhaps they would be sorry to see the humans go.

In Loraine's room on the window-seat he found her brush. He put it in his pocket and returned to the kitchen where on the dying fire he heated coffee, drank it, and ate the last of the bread and margarine. The remaining vegetables he threw out over the kitchen garden wall, blew out the candles and took them and their holders with kettle, pots and pans to the van. Lastly he bolted the back door, descended to the cellar, climbed out of the window, shut it, and wiped the dust and cobwebs from his hands.

In the van he changed into his brown suit, then, with blankets around him to keep out the cold, sat in the chair. The van he had bought for £250: surely the garage would give him more than £50? And the farmer must give him at least that for the caravan . . .

He drove away at half-past six and reached the main road at a quarter to seven. The farm was a quarter of a mile further on. He drove there slowly, and came to the farmyard, stopping near the door. The caravan didn't look too shabby, he thought, in the faint light of early morning . . . the son, Timmy, came out first.

'Oh, it's you, is it? I'll call mi dad.'

Harry waited twenty minutes. He was walking round the caravan noticing all sorts of blemishes he never knew were there when the old man came out in an old grey topcoat with a belt round the middle and an ancient hat on his head.

'Come t'pay t'reckoning then?'

'Well, yes, but I find I haven't any cash. I was wondering whether you'd buy my caravan — '

'Ah doan't want no bludy caravan!'

'Please take it. I haven't anything else . . . it's in good condition. Have a look inside — '

'It's more like a bludy hencoop in mi reckoning.'

'I'll take twenty pounds — '

'Twenty pun! Twenty pun! I'll not give thee twenty shillin'. And what would I want wi' a caravan, any road?'

'We could use it as a henhouse, Da — '

'Shut thi trap, will 'ee, thoo girt cauf'eead![1] Now then, mister, you agreed to five pun, and five pun I'll have — '

'I haven't got it.'

'Not got it? No brass at all?'

'I've just twenty pence — four shillings — '

'Fower shillin'?'

'Gi him five pun for it, Dad.'

'Sithee . . . '

---

[1] Calf head.

He looked at the caravan, peered in at the windows, walked all round it, scratching it where the paint had worn away.

'It ain't worth it — but reckon I won't see mi money, else. I'll give 'ee five pun.'

'But it's worth far more than that! I've petrol to get. I've not enough even to get to Scarborough. I need more than that — '

'Five pun, mister.'

'Make it ten — '

'I said five. Want me t'call policeman? I'll 'ave a tale to tell him, thee breakin' and enterin' t'big house.'

'But — '

The old man was peering in at the windows again. He said,

'Five pun ten shillin' — and that's all, see?'

'All right.'

'I'll go and fetch the money.'

He went indoors. Timmy said, grinning,

'Brass is brass to mi dad. Tell you

what I'll do. I'll gie 'ee a lick o' petrol
. . . but don't you tell mi dad!'

'Thank you. Thank you very much.'

Timmy went to the tractor shed and
returned with a two gallon can. He
poured it into the tank.

'Tain't high grade stuff, you'll understand — '

'It's good of you — '

'You'm leavin' just in time, mister. I
was gooin' t'tell 'ee t'other day the
place was to be brought down, but now
I hear it's let from next spring — some
daft southroners have taken it. T'owner
is in Scotland but we hear there's men
comin' in any day to put the place to
reights — '

'Letting it? It's in a shocking
state — '

'All southroners is daft,' said Timmy
from the tractor shed where he was
putting the can away. His father came
out with his wife.

'How's the babe?'

'I don't know yet.'

'Hope she'll be all reight.'

'Here you are, mister. Ten bob.'

The coin was handed over, Harry unhitched and got into the van.

'So long, mister,' said Timmy. 'Good luck.'

Harry said nothing but drove quickly away. He didn't want to look at the home he'd cast off for fifty pence.

He waited outside the Kirkland Post Office until it opened. He must try again to get some money so he bought a card and an envelope, went into a corner to write it but after a few minutes gave up. It wouldn't be any use because there was nothing the solicitors could do; they'd told him before. He was about to leave when the post-mistress came through.

'Aren't you the gentleman came in some weeks ago? Mr Hobart?'

'Yes.'

'There's some letters for your wife.'

'She's in hospital having her baby.'

'I'll give them to you if you'll sign for them.'

He put the letters in the glove pocket

240

of the van and was on his way. As he
drove he thought of the child: boy or
girl? He wondered which would please
her most — but it didn't matter, as long
as both were safe. He thought of the
father so far away neither knowing nor
caring. It was monstrous that he
shouldn't even know. He must be
written to. He must be made to pay
something. He would use the card and
envelope to write to Eric, tell him he
had a child, and that Loraine was in
need of money to pay the nursing-
home . . .

. . . he wouldn't write to Eric. Eric
was out of it. Anyway he wouldn't reply.

An hour later he was at the Wyvern.
He went in and gave his name to the
girl in Inquiries. She looked startled.

'Wait here a moment, please.'

She went away and Harry looked
around. They were always the same,
hospitals, big or small, with their smell
of disinfectant. It was a smell that made
him uneasy. A stout matron in a blue
uniform came into the hall.

'Come into my room please, Mr Hobart.'

'Yes. yes, of course . . . '

'Please sit down — '

'I'd rather stand.'

'I think you had better sit. We've bad news for you, I'm afraid.'

Harry sat slowly, colour ebbing.

'It's — it's my wife?'

'She is very, very ill. The baby, it was a girl, was born the evening Dr Wilson brought her in. Unfortunately the cord — we call it umbilical strangulation, Mr Hobart. The surgeon and the doctors did their best to get it out alive but it became a question of saving the mother. As we couldn't get in touch with you, Dr Wilson took the decision for you, but by that time she'd lost a great deal of blood. She has had a very bad haemorrhage — several.'

'Will she live?'

The matron hesitated.

'I don't want to raise your hopes, Mr Hobart. The doctor gives her a chance, but that's all. We are doing everything we can . . . '

'May I see her?'

'She's very, very ill, Mr Hobart — but of course.'

She led him along a corridor and upstairs. His feet didn't seem to be touching the ground.

'Dr Wilson will be in again soon.'

He was shown into a small ward. She was lying very still her face like wax. Blood was being transfused and a sister was wiping her forehead and her lips. He went to her.

'Loraine . . . '

Her eyes were closed. She looked already dead. He bent closer.

'Lorry . . . it's me. Harry.'

He thought there was going to be no response but after a while there was a movement of her eyelids.

'I'm here, my darling.'

Now her eyes opened a fraction, and she tried to speak. He took her hand. She whispered,

'I thought you'd deserted me.'

'As if I would . . . '

'You must come away now, Mr Hobart.'

'You'll be all right, Lorry darling. You've got to be, see?'

He thought there was a tiny pressure on his hand. He could not see clearly his way to the door.

For half-an-hour he sat in his van both hands gripping the wheel. He had looked after her for so long he couldn't believe they could save her unless he were there, and he wanted to go back to her, hold her, save her himself. Every now and then he looked up at the windows, trying to find hers, his face set as it had been when he had saved her from those lads.

When Dr Wilson arrived he saw him, came to the van.

'I'm sorry about this, Mr Hobart. We shouldn't have tried to save the baby — '

'It doesn't matter now. All that matters is that you save her. Please, please — '

'We are doing our best. You've seen her?'

'Yes.'

The doctor waited but Harry didn't say any more.

'May I suggest something?'

'Please.'

'Find a church and say a prayer.'

The doctor went into the nursing-home and after a while Harry left the van. He walked down the hill from the old castle and saw a church. It seemed to spring into his vision from nowhere. He went in. He walked slowly towards the altar, sat in a pew. Sometimes he stared at the brass-bright tabernacle, sometimes at a marble memorial nearby, but not often at the memorial for it looked too much like Loraine who had said,

'It's a load of rubbish. God had to be invented to punish people who didn't conform. Don't expect me to go to church ever.'

Was this the way God, if there were a God, treated people? By punishing

245

them if they didn't conform? Was Loraine to be punished for breaking His commandments? For calling Him a 'load of rubbish'?

It grew darker so that the only light seemed to be coming from the golden tabernacle. His hands clasped together on the back of the bench in front of him, he was leaning forward his eyes fixed on that small brightness in the gloom. He had lost his thoughts about punishment; all that was important was to ask whoever might dwell in this place that his golden sparrow should not die.

He sat in the church for two hours, then, stiff from long sitting, he left the church to find the sky leaden again and snow beginning to fall. He walked back to the Wyvern. He must take his van somewhere and sleep in it. He didn't want to go as far as Dendale, so far from her, and yet he had the feeling that it did not greatly matter where he went now. He had no certain knowledge that she would live only that the outcome was not his to decide.

He was thinking of going into the home again when Dr Wilson came out.

'So you are still here.'

The doctor put his hand on the van door, said,

'I think she's better. I believe I can give her more than a fifty-fifty chance. She has rallied quite a bit during these last two hours — she's a determined girl! Now, Mr Hobart, you'd better go and get a good rest. I'll be here again in the morning.'

He looked at the thickly falling flakes.

'If I can get!'

Dr Wilson drove off and a few minutes later Harry followed. He drove very carefully. It was important for him to live too.

16

He made no great effort to sell the van, for he found it not a proposition the Kirkland garages were interested in. A scrap merchant at Kirkland Mills offered him twelve pounds, but he reckoned it would be cheaper for him to sleep in it.

He parked it at Dendale, and kept himself by casual labour. He did what he could where he could, mostly shovelling snow.

It was two days before he could get into Scarborough and when he arrived the matron told him she was better, and that he could stay ten minues. He sat beside the bed holding her hand.

'Well, well, well! You do look better!'

'I had to get better to see your ugly mug again!'

She was still pale but the waxen image look had gone.

'I'm sorry about the baby. Has that made you very unhappy?'

'It was a girl, but I expect you know that. In a way, yes, of course. All that making all for nothing . . . but you, Harry, how are you? You look so thin.'

'I'm fine. Working. Odd jobs. Don't worry about me, my darling. You concentrate on getting well again.'

'I feel awfully weak . . . '

Her voice showed it, so he told her not to talk any more and spoke of the fun he was having in his jobs until Sister said he had had long enough.

On the Saturday morning he called at the Dendale Post Office for some sweets to give her and was handed a postcard and a typed envelope. The postcard was from Loraine, the envelope contained an invoice from the Wyvern for the week: sixty pounds. He thrust the bill out of sight and didn't ask himself how he was going to pay but read and re-read her card although there were only two lines. 'Am ever so much better. Please come soon'.

He planned to go on Sunday for the gardener at the school had given him a job for most of the Saturday; so it wasn't until he was in his van that night and undressing for his bunk that he remembered the Wyvern account. He lay awake thinking of ways of paying it or not paying it at all. By midnight he was considering putting a ladder to her window and carrying her off; was thinking of stealing back the caravan and selling it in York for a respectable sum. Or perhaps he would set fire to the school, heroically rescue all the boys and be rewarded with an enormous cheque . . . crazy plans that kept at bay of how long it would take him to save sixty pounds by casual labour.

When he saw her on the Sunday she was sitting up! She put out her arms and he came to her, kissed her; she would not let him go, so he sat beside her and they held hands and smiled like children round a Christmas tree. He asked her when she expected to leave.

'Soon, I hope. Harry, I've brought

nothing but hardship to you — '

'Nonsense, Lorry, nonsense!'

'I have, I have. Last night I asked matron what the bill would be and she said so far it was about eighty-five pounds. If I have to be here another week — '

'Don't think about it. Please don't or you won't get well.'

'All right. I'll try not to . . . what about you, Harry? How are you doing? Are you getting enough to eat?'

'Rather! The head gardener at the school, Joe Kirby, has been giving me jobs clearing the paths around the buildings, and yesterday he gave me a hot dinner — a real, fab. dinner, Lorry! Roast beef, Yorkshire pud, potatoes in their jackets, carrots and onions. I bet I had a better dinner than you did! Mr Kirby has quite restored my liking for Yorkshiremen!'

'What do you mean by that?'

He tried to wriggle out of it but she asked,

'How much did you pay the farmer

for towing us out?'

'I should never have taken you to that house. It's my fault you got so ill — '

'Come on, Harry, give. How much did you pay him?'

'I had to sell the caravan, Lorry.'

'Oh no! Not our home?'

'I had to, had to.'

'What did he give you for it?'

He examined his nails as though he had never seen them.

'Five pounds fifty. There was nothing else I could do. I'm sorry. His son gave me some petrol . . . '

She took his hand.

'Never mind, darling, no good crying over spilt milk — which reminds me, my greatest discomfort has been too much of it — but they've been doing something about that. Oh dear! Poor little old caravan . . . '

When he reached the slope down to his camping site he realized he would never get up it there was so much snow; so he parked at the top. He went to bed early to save what little power he had left in his battery and again lay awake for hours recriminating himself for parting with the caravan so easily for now Loraine would have to go to her mother who wouldn't want her, and he — what would happen to him? If he couldn't pay the nursing home he would be prosecuted and that would mean his name in the papers and . . . it was ironic that he might go to prison after all for not paying his debt.

On Monday there was heavy snow, roads blocked so that no buses ran. He fretted at being unable to visit Loraine so on the 21st decided to get to her in the van. He first shovelled a double track from top to bottom of the slope, then, heart in mouth, got the vehicle moving, jumped in, let it get up speed, pulled the choke, let in the gear — and thanked God when the engine fired. He let it warm up thoroughly before attempting the slope and while waiting opened the glove pocket to see if there were any cigarettes, and saw the two letters he had forgotten to give her. He put them in his pocket.

It took him two hours to reach Scarborough but the tribulations of the journey were forgotten when he arrived to find her dressed and sitting on the bed.

'She has made a truly wonderful recovery,' said the matron. 'We are all terribly pleased with her. Dr Wilson was saying only yesterday that he could hardly believe that ten days ago she seemed to be at death's door — you can be very proud of her, Mr Hobart.'

'I am! this is marvellous — can she go today?'

'Good gracious me, no! Not before tomorrow at the very ealiest and even then you must take the greatest care of her. We'll talk about that after you've had your time together.'

But at the door she turned and indicated to Harry to accompany her.

'I am sorry to mention this, Mr Hobart, but — well — we do have weekly terms and I had hoped that today . . . '

She looked at the frayed cuffs of his brown suit.

'Your bill now stands at over eighty pounds. Do you belong to BUPA?'

'I'm afraid not,' said Harry, wondering what that was.

'I mustn't keep you from your wife now but before you leave I would like you to come to my office.'

It was an order and Harry understood why she was a matron. He helped Loraine to walk across the room and back. It was all she could manage.

'I suppose my legs will function again one day!'

He helped her into the armchair beside the fire.

'What does matron want to see you about? Money?'

'I expect so.'

'Harry, what are you going to do?'

'I don't know, my darling. I've thought of everything I can — crazy things mostly. I even considered asking Eric to help. I've seen myself in prison for debt —'

'They don't do that these days, do they? Harry, I'm frightened — what will they do if we can't pay?'

'Take us to court, I suppose — but don't let's talk about that, sweetheart. I haven't kissed you yet.'

He knelt beside her chair, put his arms about her.

'You sure know how to kiss, Harry! Are you sure you've had no practice?'

He flushed, turned away from her.

'You look — ' she began, stopped in mid-sentence as abruptly as he had turned his back. He had gone to his overcoat, brought out two letters.

'I just remembered these letters. I ought to have given you them ages ago but I left them in the van. This one from your mother — I'm not sure you should open it.'

There was a peculiarly serene expression in her eyes when she answered.

'Nothing can hurt me now, Harry.'

She opened the one from Louth first, read it laughing.

'Sheila says she's had six first babies,

five of them boys! She sounds very cheerful.'

'You sound suddenly very cheerful yourself,' he said.

'Oh, I am!'

While Harry read Sheila's remarks about the babies and their mothers Loraine opened the one from her mother.

'Harry! Harry, listen to this: 'My dear Loraine, thank you for writing to me so nicely. I'm afraid I was a bit over-wrought the day you came with the tournament that afternoon. I'm sorry. You will have a lot of expenses with a new baby so I'm sending you a little Christmas present which I hope you will find acceptable.'

She held out a slip of paper.

'What a lot of old codswallop I did talk about parents ceasing to love their children. She's sent me a cheque for a hundred pounds.'

17

Christmas Eve and the *Pageant* was, he thought, the right time and place. The caravan — the old rogue had let him have it back for £10 — was parked on the aerodrome near Bishopsthorpe and they were sitting in a corner of the pub, which was as usual crowded with men all of them singing, the place decorated with holly and coloured streamers.

'I made you a promise — '

'You needn't keep it.'

'I must. I shouldn't feel happy if I didn't.'

'All right. But I'm going to marry you whatever you say!'

'I hope so because I think I should die if you threw me over now. But I must make my confession. You know I started a career as a teacher at Borstal. I was there for seven years. It was tough going. One never knew what the lads would be up to and sometimes they were very difficult, poor devils. In the end the job got me down so I asked to be transferred to another branch of the service, to a school approved by the Home Secretary for younger offenders. You remember the snapshots, the one you found when we were on Holme beach?'

'Yes.'

'I tore it up as you saw, and by doing that I tore up, as I soon came to see very clearly, a good deal of what was the matter with me. It was a photograph of a boy called Johnnie Appleton. He was the son of a professional wrestler and he'd been sentenced to us for window breaking. His father had beaten him for it but still he smashed windows, not merely the windows of the houses around his home but the windows of shops. No amount of punishment stopped him because it was his way of showing his hatred of the world.'

He was silent for a moment, took a sip of his beer, and continued,

'Johnnie's mother had died when he was ten: when he came to us he was thirteen and a half. He was neither handsome nor ugly — just a boy, though I think most people found him somewhat unprepossessing with his heavy, aggressive scowls. But when he smiled, there was so much gaiety on his lips and in his eyes, — not that he smiled often but when he was put in my care I made it my business to bring out that smile, and gradually the sourness in his soul ebbed away. Since his mother's death no one had given him what he so badly needed — what all young offenders need — affection.'

He put both his hands around his glass and stared into it.

'Today it all seems so remote and so absurd like that fellow who nearly a year ago sat in this pub wondering whether anyone would come to sit beside him and he would dare to talk to them: and saw a girl come in who was as stricken as Johnnie had been. I was the only person in the world who was helping him to find his way out of the darkness of his life — '

'And it didn't take him as long to love you as it did me. Right?'

He gave her a quick smile.

'Thank you for that understanding comment, Lorry . . . Late one night I woke to find him beside my bed. 'Please sir,' he said. 'I gotta brick. I wanter smash them winders. Lemme stay here with you, sir, then I won't do that'. I was going to order him back to bed but he looked so pathetic, so I sat up and patted the side of the bed and he sat down and then suddenly he was in my arms and was crying. I stroked his head and said — well, I said much the same as I said to you. I told him to cry away his hatred of the world. He cried for ten minutes — I remember my pyjama jacket was soaked — then he lifted his head, stared at me for a second through his tears, and kissed me.'

He was silent again and the singing of the men swam back surrounding them as by a roaring sea.

'The next day when he was alone with me in a classroom I told him he mustn't come to my room, but that evening he was caught outside near the greenhouses with a brick in his hands. Knowing that I'd been put in charge of him the night porter brought him to me, so he was again alone with me in my room.

'I don't know how often he came or how often I tried to stop him from coming, or how sincerely I did try. Not very sincerely because I needed affection too and — you said it — Johnnie loved me. Schoolmasters are always vulnerable to the affection of boys — but I mustn't make excuses. He came, and I let him come, let him love me, and loved him back . . .'

Now his chin had sunk to his chest as he whispered,

'I gave him the love he yearned for and came to think that this was the sort of love I needed too, that, to help them, I must give boys like Johnnie all of myself so that they would forget their hatred for the world and, like Johnnie, become gentle and friendly. And smile instead of scowl.'

He gave a small shake of his head and sighed.

'What happened next seems like what happens in a nightmare. Somebody told the head what was going on — the other boys I expect — and I was summoned to the housemaster's office. He was pretty understanding I realize now. He said I'd done good work with Johnnie but this sort of thing — he'd have to report it, that was his duty. I had nothing to say — I'd behaved abominably so there was nothing I could say. That same day, Johnnie went home. Boys who'd won good conduct marks were allowed home-leave, if their homes were suitable which many were not. While at home I can only surmise that Johnnie said something to his father about me. The obvious — well, the only — interpretation was put on it and I found myself again before the Principal. He told me Mr Appleton had 'phoned to say he was coming to give me a thrashing and would institute proceedings. The head said he would try to dissuade Mr Appleton from such a course and would in any case do his best to see that no ministerial action was taken so long as I never applied for a post in any school: and it would be better if I were out of the way when Mr Appleton came.

'I was bewildered and frightened. My job, my whole career, was smashed, and what had seemed the right way, the only way, of pulling a boy out of his misery and on to a firm basis of self-understanding, was now seen as the wrong way, as a crime, which it was.'

Loraine opened her mouth to speak but he continued,

'I left the head's room, packed a few books and clothes in a suitcase, and took a 'bus into Maidstone and from there a train to London. I didn't know where I was making for, hardly what I was doing but having started to run I went on running. I went north because having never been there I imagined the north to be a place where a man could hide. I took a ticket to Doncaster and after a night in the waiting-room had the idea of buying a caravan. At the back of my mind was the belief that if I kept constantly on the move, a person of no fixed address, my past would never catch up with me — or perhaps I was trying to escape from what I thought I'd become. One thing I did know for sure: I didn't want Johnnie dragged through a court case. Anyway, I learned that at Bawtry a few miles away there were caravans for sale. I had plenty of money for I'd saved most of my private income. I bought the caravan and the van and started my pilgrimage . . . '

Now, face set, he concluded,

'That's my story, Loraine. I — I haven't the courage to ask you to marry me now.'

She put the fingers of both hands under his chin, lifted his face so that he had to look at her.

'You're a bit of a fuddy-duddy still, Harry, my darling! Did you really expect me to be shocked? I suppose if I'd been an innocent miss of those Dotheboy novels I might have been, but I am illuminated with some knowledge of the world, you know. These things happen. I've known them happen in the hotel business where there are still page-boys and I know it is often an over affectionate boy who starts it. Besides, I guessed! I guessed when you looked so uncomfortable when I asked you if you had had any practice in kissing because I remembered that snapshot and it popped into my head that he was your secret. I ought to have told you then but like any woman I was curious to know how it had come about.

'No, my darling. I know you, you are my *man*. You've proved yourself that over and over again. So if you're not going to propose to me I'll have to propose to you.'

She made a demure face and added,

'Mr Hobart, will you do me the

honour of becoming my wedded husband?'

Her expression, her tone of voice, was so comical that tension snapped and he laughed. Then suddenly everyone was singing 'Good King Wenceslaus looked out', bawled by the crowd, Christmas cheer showing in sweating red faces and unsteady legs . . .

At eleven they left the pub arm in arm, hand holding hand, came to Lendall Bridge, and stood looking down into the black water.

'Do you remember how I said 'I wish you wouldn't keep on saying Look'?'

'Yes, you cheeky thing!'

'You don't say it at all now.'

'And you — you don't swear as much as you did. What's that a sign of?'

'Security,' she replied. 'And contentment.'

They strolled on through the blustery night to the Minster, went in, joined the packed congregation in the singing of carols. 'The Holly and the Ivy.'

'You liked being in there?' he asked

as they walked slowly back to where they'd parked the van.

'It seemed appropriate. To be with the tribe, to be one with the tribe, on a night like this.'

'But you have no use for it?'

'I don't know. Have you?'

'Yes. I prayed for you when you were nearly dying. And you got better.'

She was silent.

'You hold me in the hollow of your hand, Harry. Like Ruth — about the only Biblical character I remember!'

He understood the illusion and squeezed her hand.

They drove to their little home and undressed by the light of the stove and so stood for a while loving each other with their eyes: then close in one another's embrace, loving with their mouths and every part of their naked bodies. Two words were in their minds but neither said them: 'At last'.

18

There were formalities to be completed before their legal marriage and in Loraine's view one essential task to be undertaken. They made for Kent where Loraine stayed with her mother, and Harry in his caravan in a near-by field. The regulations were seen to in Maidstone and then, Loraine said,

'Now we are going to see Mr Appleton.'

Harry smiled.

'And if he gives me any nonsense I'll give him a piece of my mind,' said Loraine. 'And anyway, you must feel free of him. Right?

'Right.'

'I suppose he's the bloke that chased us?'

'Yes.'

'Afraid to meet him now?'

'No.'

'Where does he live?'

'Mote Park — near the cricket field.'

'Then let's go.'

On the way Loraine said,

'I'm glad I had a baby, poor little thing. A woman isn't a woman until she has had a child. So much rubbish is drained away from her at a birth. There was an awful lot of rubbish in me.'

They came to the little house. It was the hairy ape himself who opened the door.

'Yes?'

'Mr Appleton — you don't remember me?'

'I do now. It's Mr Hobart, isn't it?'

'That's right. This is my fiancée. May we come in?'

He brought them into a sitting-room full of silver trophies and photographs of himself in and out of the ring.

'Is there anything you want to say to me, Mr Appleton?'

The big man looked at Loraine, then at Harry.

'No, sir.'

'Miss Cartright knows about — about Johnnie. How is he?'

'Fine, fine. He's nearly sixteen now. Apprenticed electrician.'

'No more trouble?'

'No, sir.'

'I believe you were pretty sore at me one time — '

'That's all past and done with. As a matter of fact, I wanted to tell you so — when was it? Last September, I think. I saw you passing through Maidstone but you did a disappearing act. I've bin puzzled ever since to know where you got to.'

So that was all that chase had been about! And like the fool he had been for so long he had run away . . .

'We'll leave it at that — a disappearing act! So Johnnie is all right now?'

'I was on the wrong lines with that boy, Mr Hobart, I'm ready to admit. You put him right. I did think all sorts of things at the time but what with one thing and another — well, Johnnie helped me to change me mind because

271

whatever happened between you, the boy was all the better for it. He never looked back. I think it was a point of honour with him to behave proper, the way you'd encouraged him. I'd like to shake your hand, sir.'

Harry found the wrestler's grip painful.

'I'm glad,' he said, rubbing his fingers.

'And I'm glad for you, too, sir, with your young lady and all. Johnnie's got a girl friend now!'

'And you, Mr Appleton? How are things with you?'

'Mustn't grumble. I'm past going into the ring though. I'd be afraid of getting hurt. But I've made a lot of money in my time. I'm comfortable, and I've a job down at the cinema on the corner. They like a big man there, especially on a Saturday night when the long-haired lads come along.'

'And Johnnie's in the electricity business — it's a good trade.

He hesitated.

'Ever mention me?'

'No, sir. Never a word these twelve months. Forgotten you most likely. Kids do.'

'Yes,' said Harry. 'Kids do.'

★　★　★

They were so used to one another, had lived together happily for so long that even for Loraine their formal union before the Maidstone Registrar in the Marriage Room with its pot plants and pink carpet seemed an anticlimax. At their 'wedding breakfast' at the *Royal Star* Mrs Cartright said,

'I knew it, didn't I? I did you a good turn, Harry, when I put Loraine in your keeping!'

'Not half as good a turn as when you sent me that Christmas present — '

'That was no more than a mother should do. Now I must fly. I've a duplicate match this afternoon. Goodbye, my dears, and good luck in whatever you decide to do.'

Postscript

At one time the *White Horse* in the Weald was a country pub with only local support. Today it is known all over Kent as a good place to dine and to stay. It would not be right to advertise its locality but in the apple orchard beside it you will see a shabby caravan weathering away with, very likely, two small boys playing in it.

Those who know the licencees say they are making a big success of their pub, and the older generation, who have read the 'Dotheboy' novels, — and some of the younger who are growing tired of the neoterical — say that not only are they being successful but are likely to 'live happily ever after'.